HOWDY!

Welcome to the Circle C. My name is Andi Carter. If you are a new reader, here's a quick roundup of my family, friends, and adventures:

I'm a tomboy who lives on a huge cattle ranch near Fresno, California, in the exciting 1880s. I would rather ride my palomino mare, Taffy, than do anything else. I mean well, but trouble just seems to follow me around.

Our family includes my mother Elizabeth, my ladylike older sister Melinda, and my three older brothers: Justin (a lawyer), Chad, and Mitch. I love them, but sometimes they treat me like a pest. My father was killed in a ranch accident a few years ago.

In **Long Ride Home**, Taffy is stolen and it's my fault. I set out to find my horse and end up far from home and in a heap of trouble.

In **Dangerous Decision**, I nearly trample my new teacher in a horse race with my friend Cory. Later, I have to make a life-or-death choice.

Next, I discover I'm the only one who doesn't know the Carter **Family Secret**, and it turns my world upside down.

In **San Francisco Smugglers**, a flood sends me to school in the city for two months. My new roommate, Jenny, and I discover that the little Chinese servant-girl in our school is really a slave.

Trouble with Treasure is what Jenny, Cory, and I find when we head into the mountains with Mitch to pan for gold.

And now I may lose my beloved horse, Taffy, if I tell what I saw in **Price of Truth**.

So saddle up and ride into my latest adventure!

Andi

ANDREA CARTER AND THE

Dangerous Decision

ANDREA CARTER AND THE

Dangerous
Decision

Susan K. Marlow

Kregel Publications

Andrea Carter and the Dangerous Decision

© 2007 by Susan K. Marlow

Published by Kregel Publications, a division of Kregel, Inc., P.O. Box 2607, Grand Rapids, MI 49501.

ISBN 10: 0-8254-3357-6
ISBN 13: 978-0-8254-3357-3

Printed in the United States of America

10 11 / 5 4 3

For Kay Erickson
and her fourth-, fifth-, and
sixth-grade language arts students:
Thanks for your encouragement and enthusiastic
support for this project.

Chapter One

RACING INTO TROUBLE

San Joaquin Valley, California, Late Summer, 1880

Twelve-year-old Andrea Carter wrapped her fingers securely around the reins of her palomino mare, Taffy, and glanced at the rider to her left. A grinning, freckle-faced boy caught her look and winked mischievously. He blew a strand of straw-colored hair from his forehead and tightened his grip on his own mount—a large chestnut gelding.

"I'm gonna beat you today, Andi," the boy challenged. "I can't hold my head up in this town no more—not since the Fourth of July." He leaned over the side of his horse and lowered his voice so that only Andi could hear. "You winning that race was nothin' but luck. And I'm gonna prove it."

Andi tossed one of her thick, dark braids behind her shoulder and laughed. She fixed a bright blue gaze on the boy. "Oh, Cory! Your chestnut couldn't beat Taffy in July, and he can't beat her now. I don't know why I let you talk me into this."

"Because you like to race as much as I do," Cory shot back. He turned to a dark-haired boy standing on the ground beside the horses. "You ready, Jack?"

Jack Goodwin nodded. He stepped up onto the corner of a nearby watering trough and balanced himself carefully. In a loud, clear voice he announced the coming race. "Ladies and gentlemen of Fresno!"

A few curious citizens stopped at the sound of the boy's voice.

When they realized the race involved nothing more than some idle youths wasting time, they shook their heads and continued down the boardwalk.

"Get on with it, Jack!" a tall, redheaded boy called from across the dusty street, where a handful of local children had gathered to watch the race. "It's hot out here."

"Aw, keep your shirt on!" the young announcer shouted back. He cupped his hands to his mouth and continued his speech. "This race is for the 1880 fall championship of the county. Riding the impressive chestnut gelding, Flash, is Cory Blake. Cory's pa runs the best livery in the whole valley. He—"

"We know who's riding Flash," the red-haired boy heckled. There was laughter from the bystanders.

"You keep quiet, Seth," Jack ordered. "I'm puttin' up the prize money, so I can do the announcin' any way I like." He raised his voice. "Next to Cory, riding the beautiful palomino mare, Taffy, is Andi Carter. Most of you know her folks own the biggest spread around these parts. Finest horseflesh in—"

"You talk too much," Cory interrupted impatiently.

"Please, Jack," Andi pleaded. "It's mighty hot."

"Oh, all right," Jack muttered unhappily. He took a deep breath and looked at the two young riders. "Listen up. The race is just a short loop around town. It starts right here, in front of the mercantile. Turn right on Tulare and head out of town 'til you come to Kincaid Vineyards. Snatch a bandana from Peter and head back to town, past the schoolhouse. Then, turn right on J. I'll be here with the prize for the winner." He held up a silver coin and raised his voice. "A dime's-worth of anything in my pa's store!" There were cheers and shouts from everyone but Andi and Cory.

Jack jumped down from the wooden trough, bowed dramatically for his audience, and lifted his arm. "Go!" he shouted, dropping his arm to his side.

Flash and Taffy leaped forward as one, surrounded by shouts and squeals of laughter from the sidelines. Joy surged through Andi as she nudged her horse into a gallop. Cory was absolutely right. She loved to race. There was nothing she would rather do. She didn't care if the sun beat down unmercifully on her bare head or the wind against her face felt hotter than a blacksmith's forge. She was racing, and she was going to win!

The businesses along J Street blurred together into one long, continuous streak of boards and brick. The two-story Arlington Hotel blended quickly into the hardware store and pharmacy. The Sequoia Bar and Restaurant appeared as a smudge of glass and color as Andi and Cory raced by, neck-to-neck.

Cory swerved to avoid an old buckboard driven by a local farmer, giving Andi an unexpected advantage. The red-faced driver stood up from his seat and raised his fist at the two young riders. He shouted something Andi couldn't make out, which was probably just as well.

She passed the newspaper office of the *Fresno Weekly Expositor* and got ready for the turn that would take her out of town and past the neighboring vineyards and orchards of the valley. She heard the sound of hoofbeats gaining on her. Cory was making up for his unexpected interruption.

"Come on, Taffy," Andi urged her horse. She knew Cory was partly right about the Fourth of July. Sometimes luck *did* play an important part in a horse race. Cory's gelding wasn't named Flash for nothing. He could very easily gain the lead. She mustn't let her guard down for an instant.

Making the turn onto Tulare Street, Andi pulled a little ahead of her opponent. A finger of worry tickled at the back of her mind. Racing down this particular street was risky. She'd have to pass right by her brother's law office. Although Justin was remarkably patient with her most days, she doubted he would approve of her racing through town at breakneck speed. If he noticed, he'd probably send her back to the ranch with a few choice words about the proper conduct for young ladies visiting town.

Before she knew it, the danger of discovery was past and she was heading out of town. Cory galloped up beside her, gave her a cheerful wave, and pulled out ahead. Andi leaned forward and willed Taffy to catch up. They were neck-to-neck again when the Kincaid Vineyards came into sight.

Andi reined Taffy to a dead stop in front of a tall, grinning youth. Without a word, she snatched the bandana from Peter's hand and drew Taffy around in a sharp pivot. Cory was right beside her on Flash. She could hear him pleading with his horse to go faster.

"Come on, Taffy," Andi encouraged her mount. "You can beat that ol' gelding any day." The palomino leaped ahead, gaining speed on the flat stretch of road that led back into town.

In no time, Andi found herself in the lead, racing down the final stretch of the course. She flew past Davy Cooper, who was sitting on the steps of the two-story schoolhouse, looking bored. He jumped up when he spotted the riders and waved his encouragement. Then he hurried away toward the finish line.

Andi glanced over her shoulder and flashed Cory a smug grin. He'd never catch her now. It was only a few more blocks.

"Andi! Look out!"

Cory's shout sliced through Andi's triumph. She whirled and gasped, "Whoa, Taffy!" At the same time, she gave the reins a frantic jerk.

Taffy planted her hooves in the dusty street and nearly sat down. A thick cloud of fine yellow dust rose up and engulfed both horse and rider. The mare struggled to regain her footing, then reared up with a frightened whinny.

"Easy, girl," Andi reassured her horse with a pat. "Settle down."

Taffy snorted and tossed her head. Her hooves crashed to the ground only inches from a figure sprawled in the middle of the street.

It was a man. He lay on his back with his eyes squeezed shut and his arms flung across his forehead as if warding off a blow. Two traveling satchels lay open beside him, with books and papers scattered in disarray. Already, a few sheets of paper were drifting away on the afternoon breeze.

"Oh, *no!*" Andi slid from the saddle and dropped down beside the man. "Are you all right, mister?" she choked out, waving away the dust. Her heart raced.

Slowly, as if he couldn't believe he had escaped death, the stranger lowered his arms and opened his eyes. He didn't seem to notice Andi kneeling beside him. His hands trembled as he pulled himself to a sitting position. He moaned softly and shook his head.

Cory ran up. "Is he hurt?"

"I don't know. He hasn't said anything yet." She laid a tentative hand on the man's arm and gave him a gentle shake. "I'm really sorry, mister. Can I help you up?"

The man blinked and seemed to come to himself. He narrowed his eyes and yanked his arm from Andi's touch. "Let me be, you young hooligan!" he snapped, suddenly alert.

Andi rose and stepped back in alarm. The bandana she'd been clutching fell from her hand. "Are you hurt? Do you want me to run for the doctor?"

"Certainly not." The man struggled to his feet and began brushing dust from his well-tailored, dark blue suit coat. He coughed, took a few cautious steps, and let out a relieved breath. "No bones broken," he muttered, glaring at Andi. "No thanks to *you*. Is this the usual welcome a stranger receives in this town?"

"It was an accident," Andi explained quickly. She picked up a book, dusted it off, and held it out. "Honest. I didn't mean to run you down. We were racing and—"

"Shame on you!" He snatched the book from Andi's hand and stuffed it into his satchel. "No reputable family would allow a girl to make such a spectacle of herself—racing publicly through the streets, trampling innocent bystanders." He brought his dust-caked face close to Andi's. "Do you realize I could have been killed?"

Staring into the man's dark, frightened eyes, Andi felt sick. It was true. Another step or two, and Taffy would have run right over the top of him. She swallowed her distress and whispered, "Yes, sir. I'm sorry."

The stranger snorted his opinion of Andi's apology. Then he reached down and began gathering up his scattered papers. "Rowdy, undisciplined youngsters. The sheriff will certainly hear about this."

Andi felt a tug on her shirtsleeve.

"Let's get out of here," Cory hissed in her ear. "He's not hurt. He just needs a chance to simmer down." He edged closer to his horse, pulling Andi along.

Trembling, Andi mounted Taffy and gave her a nudge. The mare broke into a trot.

"Stop!" the stranger bellowed. "How dare you run away!"

Andi hesitated. She watched Cory gallop down the street to safety. Then she glanced over her shoulder to see the man snatch up his satchels and stomp off toward the schoolhouse. He disappeared inside the building, slamming the door shut.

Andi urged Taffy into a canter. "We're in a heap of trouble," she announced when she caught up to Cory. "We shouldn't have run away. When Sheriff Tate finds out and tells our folks . . ." Her voice trailed away in misery.

Cory slowed his horse to a walk. "He doesn't know who we are. Besides, it was an accident. Give him a day or two and he'll forget all about it."

"He went into the schoolhouse," Andi said. "You don't suppose—"

"Don't even think it," Cory said, cutting her off. "He can't be the new schoolmaster. Your brother wouldn't agree to hire such a bad-tempered man . . . would he?"

Andi didn't know, nor did she care to guess what Justin and the school board had been up to this summer. "But what if he is?" she persisted.

Cory sighed. "If he is, then you're right. We are in a *lot* of trouble."

Chapter Two

RELUCTANT STUDENT

The first day of school dawned clear, bright, and hot. It was a beautiful morning, but Andi didn't notice. She hadn't noticed much of anything for the past week. She was too busy trying to figure out a way she could avoid the fall term of school—and the new teacher. She had yet to come up with a plan her mother might believe. Her offer to stay home and help put up the fall harvest had fallen on deaf ears.

"I thought offering to peel hundreds of apples was a pretty good idea, Taffy." Andi leaned against her horse and sighed. She'd managed to slip away to the barn after breakfast for an early morning conference with her friend. "But Mother just smiled her I-know-what-you're-thinking smile and said I could help on Saturdays." She reached into her dress pocket and pulled out a handful of hard, white lumps. "Here. I brought you a treat."

Taffy greedily accepted the offering of sugar, devouring it in one quick bite. She nuzzled Andi's hand, as if hoping to find another treat. When no more tasty white lumps appeared, the mare shook her head. Her ivory mane went flying into Andi's face.

She brushed it aside. "Oh, Taffy! What if the man I nearly trampled turns out to be the new teacher? I can't face him. I've got to figure out some way of staying home this morning." Resting her head against Taffy's warm flank, she closed her eyes and tried desperately to come up with a plan. She knew she didn't have much time. Any minute now, Justin would be along to drive her to school. *Let's see. I could jump off the barn roof and break a—*

"It's time to go, Andi."

Andi's eyes flew open. She pushed away from Taffy and faced her oldest brother, who was leaning over the half door of the stall. "So soon? Couldn't I stay home a couple more days?"

"Nope," Justin replied crisply. "Mother made it perfectly clear at breakfast this morning. Let's not go over it again, please."

Andi sighed unhappily. It was clear that Justin was in no mood to sympathize with her. She threw her arms around Taffy's neck. "I'll be back this afternoon," she whispered into the mare's ear. "If it's not too hot, we'll go for a long ride."

With a final wave to her best friend, Andi shuffled out of the stall, latched the bottom half of the door, and followed Justin outside. She blinked as rays of early morning sunlight struck her in the face. The day held the promise of unrelenting heat.

She glanced with longing at her family's Spanish-style ranch house. Its white stucco walls glistened in the morning sun. The red-tiled roof added a splash of color to the brown and barren landscape of a dusty California summer. Huge valley oaks and well-watered gardens surrounded the house and many of the outbuildings, offering a refreshing place to rest and relax during the heat of the day. To exchange this pleasant setting for the inside of a town building was the last thing Andi wanted to do this morning—or any morning.

"Hey, Andi! You look like you're on your way to prison," a cheerful voice called out from across the yard.

Andi looked around. Her other two brothers, Chad and Mitch, stood near the far corral, saddling their horses and talking together. "I am," she shouted back. She ran over to the corral. "You should've been at breakfast, when Mother handed down the sentence."

"What you need is a good lawyer, sis," Mitch said, planting his wide-brimmed hat firmly onto his blond head. "Maybe you can ask Justin to appeal your case."

"Not likely," Andi replied sourly. "He's on Mother's side." She stepped onto the bottom railing and peered into the corral where the working horses were kept. Half a dozen cowhands were roping and saddling their mounts for the day. They all wore expressions of excitement and expectation. "Where are you off to?"

"Some of us are going after the rogue stallion," Mitch said. "Chad's bound and determined to get those mares back."

Andi whirled to face her brothers. She ignored Justin's loud warning that she would be late for school. "You mean that big, dappled gray fella who's been running around the range like he owns it?"

"That's the one," Chad said. He finished cinching up his saddle and turned around. His blue eyes flashed. "That maverick's stolen his last mare."

Andi jumped down from the fence. "Golly, I wish I could go along."

"Sorry, Andi." Chad swung into his saddle. "Maybe some other time."

"Is Melinda going?" she asked with a twinge of envy.

A quiet chuckle relieved Andi's fear that her older sister might accompany the men on their search for the stallion. "Melinda says it's too hot to go chasing after wild horses," Mitch said, pushing back his hat. He leaned toward Andi and lowered his voice in warning. "Justin looks a mite impatient, sis. You'd better go before he comes after you."

Andi tried to hide her disappointment at being left out of what was sure to be an exciting day on the ranch. Why had Chad picked *today* of all days to go after the stallion and his stolen band of mares? She turned away from the men and kicked angrily at a rock. A small cloud of fine dust billowed up, then settled quickly onto her newly polished, high-top black shoes. When she looked up, she saw Justin shaking his head. She hastily bent down, brushed the dust from her shoes, and hurried over to the buggy. Her brother didn't say a word as he helped her into the rig.

A slender, pretty Mexican girl about Andi's age was waiting in the buggy when Andi climbed in. The girl's shiny black hair was twisted into a long braid, tied at the end with a red ribbon. Her dark eyes danced with excitement. She greeted Andi with a smile and a cheery *buenos días*.

"Hi, Rosa," came Andi's less-than-cheerful reply.

"Are you feeling better about going to school?" Rosa chattered away in Spanish. "I couldn't help overhearing the argument this morning when *Mamá* and I were serving breakfast."

Andi slid over and made room for Justin, who immediately flicked the reins. The horse took off at a lively trot. "No," she replied. "I feel worse than ever. I just learned that Chad and Mitch are going after Whirlwind."

Rosa wrinkled her forehead in confusion. "Whirlwind?"

"That's what I named the stallion that showed up a few weeks ago. None of the ranchers will claim him. Nobody knows where he's from, but he's bent on gathering up every mare on the range. I've seen him a couple of times. He's fast as the wind. It sure would be something to watch the boys catch him."

"*Sí*," Rosa agreed loyally. "I am sure it would be."

Andi grinned and squeezed her friend's hand. She knew Rosa had no interest in horses. With a quick glance at her brother, Andi leaned closer to Rosa and said, "I bet if Father were alive, he'd let me skip a day of school to go after Whirlwind with the boys."

"No, he wouldn't," Justin announced gravely, in English.

Andi opened her mouth to argue, but quickly changed her mind. Arguing with Justin never got her anywhere. He spent his days arguing cases in court and knew all the tricks. She was better off saying nothing at all.

Justin gave the horse a slap of the reins. "Andi, up until a week ago, you and Rosa were all fired up about the new term. Now you want to back out. That's not like you. Is something bothering you?"

Andi shook her head. It was no use. No matter how hard she tried to feel excited about school for Rosa's sake, her stomach churned at the thought of meeting the new teacher. She sat stiffly between Rosa and Justin, her hands clenched tightly in her lap. She didn't feel like talking anymore.

The hour-long trip into Fresno, which on other days flew by, dragged. Finally, Justin pulled up next to the schoolyard and brought the buggy to a halt. "Well, here you are, girls. Come down to my office after school and I'll give you a ride home."

"*Gracias, Señor* Justin," Rosa said cheerfully. She reached for his hand and jumped lightly from the buggy.

Andi let Justin help her down. She landed on the ground and looked up in surprise. Justin was holding tightly to her hand and regarding her with his serious, I-want-to-talk-to-you expression.

"What's the matter?" Andi glanced around for Rosa, but her friend had moved off a discreet distance to wait.

Justin released her hand. "That's what I'd like to know. There's something troubling you. I've noticed lately that every time the subject of school comes up, you look ready to run for your life. Why?"

Andi shrugged and stared at the ground. *I should tell him. I really should*. But the words stuck in her throat. "I heard there's a new teacher," she said instead.

Justin nodded. "You heard right. So?"

Andi glanced up at the large, two-story schoolhouse and made a face. "I don't want a new teacher." The memory of her regrettable encounter with the man settled in her stomach like a lump of cold, soggy oatmeal.

"You begged for a new teacher all last term," Justin reminded her. "I seem to recall hearing about spit wads, peashooters, and Johnny Wilson at least once a week."

Andi frowned in remembrance. Before she could say anything, Justin went on.

"Things are going to be different this year. The school board decided to divide the school and hire a new teacher. Miss Hall will continue to instruct the little ones, while the new schoolmaster, Mr. Foster, will manage you older, more challenging students upstairs. He assured us that he will restore order and discipline—something that's been sorely lacking these past two years."

"I don't want a mean, strict schoolmaster."

"Behave yourself, and you won't have a thing to worry about," he shot back. Then he grinned and tweaked one of Andi's long, dark curls. "Don't fret, honey. Mr. Foster seems like a fair and honest man. Perhaps a little more straitlaced than you and your friends are used to, but he's from the East. He'll learn our ways, and you'll adjust."

Andi wasn't so sure about that. A city-slicker Easterner trying to manage a classroom full of ranchers' and farmers' kids? He was in for a surprise.

"Mr. Foster has a daughter," Justin said.

That brought Andi up short. "A daughter?"

"Two, in fact. I met the girl your age when Mr. Foster came by the office to sign his contract. Seems like a nice, quiet young lady. I suggested that perhaps you two could become acquainted." He paused, as if expecting a response.

"Uh, sure, Justin," Andi said quickly.

Justin sighed. "Listen, Andi. Mr. Foster left a good-paying position as headmaster of a prominent school back East to move his family out here, for health reasons. It's been a hard adjustment for them, so I don't want you giving the man any trouble."

Andi cringed. She never purposely gave *anyone* trouble. Trouble just seemed to follow her around—like last Saturday's disaster.

Justin was still talking. "Mr. Foster's going to have his hands full as it is." He picked up the *Expositor*, which lay in his lap, and handed it to her. "Take a look at the story near the bottom of the page. It's not the welcome I would have chosen."

Andi took the newspaper and began reading. "'From Gerald Foster, our new schoolmaster, we learn that quite an excitement was stirred up the other day down in front of the grammar school. It appears that a couple of young rowdies gave the teacher an unforgettable welcome to our fair city by nearly stampeding him with their horses. Mr. Foster has taken the matter up with the sheriff and hopes to quickly identify and bring the offenders before Judge Morrison on a charge of . . .'"

Andi caught her breath in disbelief. "Malicious mischief!" She swallowed and tossed the paper into Justin's lap. She couldn't read any more.

Justin folded the paper. "I told Sheriff Tate that my money's on the Hollister kids. They're a wild bunch and wouldn't think twice before tearing through town on their horses. They'd consider roughing up the new schoolmaster to be great sport." He shook his head. "And the Hollister kids are the least of his problems. There's Johnny Wil—"

"It wasn't Sadie and Zeke Hollister," Andi blurted out, before she changed her mind.

"Oh?" Justin raised his eyebrows in interest. "You know who it was?"

Andi nodded miserably. "It was . . . it was . . . Cory and me." She swallowed. "Mostly it was me."

"No!"

"It was an accident," she explained in a rush of words. "I didn't see him. Honest, I didn't. It happened so fast. He came out of nowhere. But you should've seen Taffy! She can stop on a dime. And a good thing, too. Not a hoof touched Mr. Foster. He was mostly . . ." She paused at the dismay written all over Justin's face. "Well," she offered in a tiny voice, "it could have been worse."

Justin grunted his opinion of that. He sat motionless, staring at the newspaper lying in his lap.

"Justin? Say something," Andi pleaded.

"What do you want me to say? The *Expositor* made light of the incident, but it's no joke. You've certainly gotten yourself into a fix *this* time."

Andi hung her head. "I know, and I'm sorry. But I have an idea. Let me wait in your office while you write up some fancy legal papers to convince Mr. Foster to drop the charges." She looked up. "You can do that, can't you?"

"Not today, I'm afraid. Preparing Jed Hatton's defense is taking all my time. The trial's only a few weeks away."

Andi sighed her impatience. "He killed Mr. Slater, Justin. He's just a dirty old drifter who—"

"Who is innocent until proven guilty," Justin said. Then he frowned. "Don't listen to gossip, Andi. It's dangerous and stirs folks up. Next thing you know they turn into a lynch mob." He lifted the reins in dismissal. "If I find the time, I'll see what I can do to help you out, but for now you'll just have to go to school and make the best of it."

He chirruped to the horse and drove away, leaving Andi standing in the street.

Chapter Three

THE NEW TEACHER

Y ou look terrible," Rosa remarked with a frown, joining Andi. "What did *Señor* Justin say to you?" She shaded her eyes and watched the buggy turn the corner onto J Street. Then she looked at Andi. "Are you in trouble again?"

Andi took a deep breath. "The worst ever." She quickly told her friend about her encounter with the new teacher.

Rosa's dark eyes widened as she listened to Andi's tale. "*¡Qué terrible!*" she said when Andi had finished. "What will you do?"

"I don't know." She crossed the schoolyard and paused near the bottom of the steps. There was no sense going into class before the bell rang. Perhaps if she stayed hidden in the crowd, she would go unnoticed by the teacher.

She glanced around the yard. No one seemed eager to enter the schoolhouse. An impromptu game of baseball was in full swing on the far side of the building. The yard in front was filled with jump ropes and colorful skirts. Andi didn't feel like joining them. Instead, she settled herself on the steps and rested her chin in her hands.

"When do we go into the school?" Rosa asked, gazing up at the silent bell tower above the double doors.

Rosa's question reminded Andi that it was her friend's first day of school. She set aside her own worries and laid a reassuring hand on Rosa's arm. "Not until the bell rings. It won't be long." She smiled. "You'll catch up fast in your lessons, so don't worry. After all, haven't I been teaching you English all summer? Just remember one thing. . . ."

Andi held up a warning finger. "The minute we step through these doors, we can't speak Spanish."

Rosa sighed. "English is so difficult. Maybe I can speak Spanish with you—if I speak quietly?"

Andi shook her head. "You can't, or we'll both be in trouble. Miss Hall was strict about this being an American school, and I'm sure Mr. Foster will be just as strict." She held Rosa's troubled look, and a sudden stab of uncertainty made her pause. Although Justin had assured her that Rosa could attend school, he'd added that it wouldn't be easy for many of the students to overlook the fact that Rosa was Mexican. *Unfair!* Andi had wanted to shout, but she knew Justin was telling her the truth. "Don't forget," she urged Rosa. "You must speak English."

At that moment, the school bell rang. Andi jumped up and grabbed Rosa's hand. They stepped aside as a crowd of noisy boys swarmed up the wide front steps and disappeared through the doors.

"Let's wait for the girls," Andi told Rosa. She waved to her friends, Rachel and Maggie, who hurried over.

"Hi, Andi." Rachel's blue eyes sparkled with curiosity. "Is this Rosa?" When Andi nodded, Rachel gave the Mexican girl a tentative smile. "I'm glad Andi talked you into coming to school."

Maggie linked an arm with Rosa and gave her a squeeze. "I'm glad, too. Our class can never have too many girls. I hope you stay all term."

"*Graci*—thank you," Rosa said, catching herself. Together, the girls climbed the wide steps and entered the schoolhouse.

"Mornin', Andi," Cory called out. He was leaning against the wall at the bottom of a narrow staircase that led to the classroom above. He folded his arms across his chest and grinned. "Ready to meet the new teacher?"

Andi stopped short. For a few minutes, she'd forgotten her own anxiety. Now it returned in full force. She looked at Rosa. "Go on up with Rachel and Maggie. I'll be along in a minute." She watched the three girls start up the stairs, then turned and faced Cory. "How can you be so cocksure of yourself?" she demanded. "Don't you know Mr. Foster's got the sheriff looking all over town for the kids who trampled him?"

Cory swiped at the hank of straw-colored hair hanging over his forehead and dug his hands deep into his pockets. "'Course I know. I saw the paper. But I heard he thinks it's the Hollister kids. I've got a notion to let him go on thinking that."

"That's fine for *you*," Andi said hotly. "All boys in overalls look pretty much alike. But what about *me*?"

"He'll never guess it was you. You're all slicked up like a proper girl today. He's looking for a wild ruffian in faded riding clothes, not a pretty girl in a new dress, who just happens to be a Carter, besides." He gave her a wide, admiring smile. "You got nothin' to worry about."

Andi felt her cheeks redden at her friend's words. "Oh, Cory, stop it!" But her spirits rose. Perhaps there was some truth to Cory's silly talk. She did look different from the dusty and frightened girl who'd nearly run over the new schoolmaster the week before. Maybe he wouldn't recognize her, and the whole regrettable incident could fade away like a bad dream. She tossed an unruly lock of dark hair behind her shoulder and gave her friend a heartfelt smile. "You sure know how to cheer a person up."

"Great," Cory said happily. "Now, take a look at this." He fumbled around in his pocket and drew out the slender thread of a writhing black and red snake. Its tiny forked tongue flicked a warning. "It's for you, Andi. First day of school wouldn't be the same if I didn't bring you a present." He kept a tight grip on the twisting baby reptile and shoved it toward her.

Andi slapped it away. "Not this year, Cory. I don't want any snakes in my desk—today or any day. Justin says this new teacher is no Miss Hall. He catches you or me with a snake or a frog or any crawly bug, and it'll be more than the corner for us. Now, get rid of it." She turned her back on him and scurried up the steps.

Cory just laughed and hurried after her.

When Andi reached the top of the stairs, she turned into the classroom and glanced around. Mr. Foster was nowhere in sight. She let out a grateful sigh and relaxed. Then she looked for her friends. She spotted them near the center of the room, giggling together. Rosa was smiling.

"Did you save me a seat?" Andi called, beginning to wind her way through the crowd. She was brought to an abrupt halt when one of the older boys, who was sprawled in a far back seat, lifted his leg and slammed a boot down on a desk, blocking her way.

"I hear your brother's defending that killer, Jed Hatton," he said. "Why would he do such a fool thing?"

Andi bristled and rushed to Justin's defense. "Not that it's any of your business, Johnny Wilson, but Justin says Jed's innocent." She gave him her fiercest look. "Now let me pass."

Johnny grinned maliciously, moved his leg barely enough to let her by, and blew her a mocking kiss. Snickers from Johnny's friends followed her up the aisle, but she ignored them the best she could. Maybe there was sense in having a mean, strict teacher after all, if he could tame the classroom bullies.

Then she forgot about Johnny as Rachel showed her the seat she'd saved. "You and Rosa can sit right in front of Maggie and me."

Andi was pleased. It was one of the best seats in class—far enough away to be out from under the schoolmaster's critical gaze, yet not so near the back of the room to become a target for the pranks of the classroom bullies. She smiled her thanks and slid into the double seat. Rosa joined her.

Cory threw himself into an empty desk across from Andi and grumbled, "I'd like to knock that ol' Johnny Wilson clean into the next county."

"You tried that last term, and he gave you a black eye and a bloody nose," Andi reminded her friend. "He's older than you, and bigger."

"Maybe I should give him a little surprise." Cory wiggled his hand in his pocket, where the snake lay trapped.

"What a nasty idea! I wouldn't do that to any creature I liked. Johnny would kill it for sure."

"Well, then, since you feel so sorry for my little friend"—he drew the snake from his pocket—"you'd best keep him safe for me." Before Andi could protest, he opened the lid of her desk, dropped the snake in, and slammed it shut with a satisfying *bang*. "Thanks a heap, Andi. You're a real chum." He gave her a wink, darted down the aisle, and slid into the seat next to Jack Goodwin. "By the way—welcome back to school."

Andi exchanged a horrified look with her seatmate. Rosa's face had gone white. "I'm sorry, Rosa. Don't panic. I'll get rid of it at recess. It's just that Cory's brought me a snake the first day of school ever since I can remember. It's tradition."

Rosa shook her head and muttered in Spanish, "A very strange tradition."

The second bell rang.

A few moments later, the new schoolmaster entered the classroom. Andi never would have guessed it was the same man she had almost trampled. For one thing, he was taller than she remembered. He marched confidently up the aisle with long, purposeful strides. No dust covered his neatly pressed dark pants and waistcoat. No fear showed in his stern, unsmiling face. Not a hair was misplaced, not a button undone. He stood in front of his desk and studied his new students with dark gray eyes.

"I am Mr. Foster, your new schoolmaster," he said when the room had quieted. "The school board warned me that this is a rowdy class. I am here to see that it is rowdy no longer." He crossed his arms over his chest and set his lips in a thin, grim line, as if daring anyone to disagree.

Andi chanced a quick glance at the boys from the corner of her eye. Every boy sat ramrod straight, gazes locked on Mr. Foster. Even Johnny Wilson looked subdued.

Mr. Foster took his place behind his desk and began speaking. "You will conduct yourselves as ladies and gentlemen at all times—both inside the classroom and after hours." He held up his hand and began ticking off on his fingers, "Truthfulness, honesty, punctuality, cleanliness, and kindness to others will be the ambition of our class, along with the highest standards of academic achievement. To achieve these goals, I have drawn up a list of rules." He called to the back of the room. "Virginia, if you would bring me the list?"

Forty heads twisted around. A young girl stood near the top of the stairs, quietly surveying the classroom. She clutched a paper in her small, pale hand.

"This is my daughter, Virginia," Mr. Foster said with a smile. "She will be joining us this term. You will find her to be a fine pupil and a capable tutor, should any of you need help in your studies. I trust you will do your best to make her feel welcome." He motioned his daughter forward.

Virginia Foster glided to the front of the classroom, handed her father the list of conduct rules, and turned to face her new classmates. She curtsied. "I'm pleased to make your acquaintance," she said in a low, soft voice.

Her greeting was met with absolute silence.

"Do none of you know how to make your manners?" Mr. Foster asked, clearly astonished.

Andi knew how, but she didn't want to bring attention to herself. So she sat and studied Virginia, instead. The teacher's daughter was thin and pallid, with hair so white, it looked like a fluff of clouds around her head. Her eyebrows were nearly invisible against her colorless face. Only her eyes showed color—the same striking dark gray as her father's. She wore a simple frock of yellow and green calico.

Walter Hancock's drawl pulled Andi's attention back to class. "I guess we ain't much for fancy ways around here." He stood up and gave Virginia a cocky bow. "Howdy, Ginny."

Virginia's cheeks flushed a delicate pink, and her lower lip quivered.

"Surely the class can do better than that," Mr. Foster exclaimed.

One by one, a few of the girls stood up, dropped a quick curtsy, and returned to their seats. After a few minutes, Mr. Foster seemed to give up. "All right, then. I will begin class by reading the rules. Later, I will post them on the back wall."

"Next to the stairs," Andi noted quietly to Rosa. "That way we can't help but see them every time we go in and out."

Mr. Foster quickly went over the rules, dropped the paper onto his desktop, and looked at his class. "I will also manage this class by assigning seats. The school board drew up a list of names and helped me place you pupils in seats that would be most beneficial to your learning."

The room exploded into groans and catcalls.

"No fair!"

"Miss Hall never—"

"Silence!" The teacher picked up a ruler and slammed it down on his desk. "I will tolerate no disrespect toward the school board's decision in this matter. Listen as I call your names and direct you to your seats."

The next few minutes erupted into noisy chaos while the new schoolmaster attempted to put his rowdy class in order. At first, Virginia looked bewildered at the confusion, but it wasn't long before she gathered herself together and moved up the aisle. She stopped beside Andi and said, "It appears that my father has assigned me this seat."

Andi exchanged a long, meaningful look with Virginia, then slid out of her seat and motioned for Rosa to do the same. *Miss Virginia Foster might look and act like the correct, gentle little lady on the outside,*

Andi decided, *but I bet she's not as shy and quiet as she lets on. She sure figured out how to wrangle the best seat in the classroom.* She watched Rachel and Maggie take their seats in front of Johnny Wilson and Walter Hancock. Too bad for her friends. Johnny was the biggest bully in the—

"I've chosen a seat especially for you."

Andi spun and faced Mr. Foster. "For me?"

He nodded. "Do you think I don't recognize you, Sadie Hollister, as the ill-mannered hooligan who nearly ended my life the other day?" He grasped Andi by the arm, propelled her to the front of the room, and thrust her into the first desk. "You will sit right here, where I can keep an eye on you. Now . . . where's your unruly brother?" He frowned. "After school, we'll visit the sheriff."

"Sadie . . . *Hollister?*" Andi's heart sank. So much for Cory's silly notion that she wouldn't be recognized. She heard a snicker from a nearby student, and her face flamed. "I'm not Sadie. The Hollisters hardly ever come to school."

A look of confusion replaced the teacher's scowl. "I was told it was most likely the Hollister youngsters who . . ." His voice trailed off, and the scowl returned. "Well, then! What *is* your name?"

Andi swallowed. "Andrea Carter."

"Carter, Carter," the schoolmaster muttered, consulting his list. His frown deepened. "Carter as in Justin Carter, one of our school trustees?"

"He's my brother," Andi reluctantly admitted.

"I'm sure you make your family very proud." Mr. Foster's mocking words felt like a slap in Andi's face. Then he abruptly changed the subject. "It appears that you're sitting over there, along with a Mexican girl." The teacher pointed to the double seat in front of Cory and shook his head. "You are not starting out the term well, young lady—if I can call you that. Don't think for one minute I've forgotten the way you welcomed me to your town."

"No, sir. It won't happen again."

"I dare say it won't. Now, go find your seat before I forget your name is Carter and punish you as you deserve."

"Yes, sir!" Andi jumped up and scurried across the room. She slipped into the empty seat in front of Cory and his friend, Jack Goodwin. Then she waved Rosa over. "You're sitting with me."

Rosa slipped into her seat and regarded Andi with dark, troubled eyes. "I do not like this American school, *mi amiga*. The school-master—he speaks fast, with words I do not understand. Perhaps it is better if I stay home."

Andi gripped Rosa's hand. "Please stay, Rosa. It'll get better." She managed a grin. "It can't get much worse."

Suddenly, from the middle of the room came a shriek of pure ter-ror. Andi caught her breath at the frightening sound.

Before she could discover what was wrong, Cory jabbed her be-tween the shoulder blades. "I think the teacher's kid just found your welcome-back gift."

Chapter Four

FROM BAD TO WORSE

Andi didn't think anyone could run as fast as Virginia Foster ran during the next ten seconds. She tore down the aisle and scrambled onto the top of the teacher's desk. There she cowered, shrieking. Andi watched in astonishment. For a dainty, quiet young lady, Virginia sure could holler!

The class burst into a tumult of shouts and laughter. Cory fell from his chair, holding his stomach and howling with glee at this unexpected distraction. Patricia Newton sat in her seat, pointing toward the desk and screaming. Others jumped up from their seats and yelled, "What happened? What's going on?"

"Silence!" Mr. Foster bellowed, coming to life with all the fire of an avenging angel. He lifted his ruler into the air and brought it crashing down against an empty front row desk. The laughter died away until Virginia's wail was the only sound in the classroom.

The teacher reached up and gathered Virginia into his arms. "Hush, daughter. There is never a good reason to act with such an unladylike display." He lowered her to the floor. "Tell me what happened."

Virginia's shrieks subsided into hysterical sobbing. "There's a . . . huge creature . . . slithering in my desk," she exclaimed between sobs. "It's horrible." She choked back a cry and covered her face with her hands. "How could anyone be so cruel?"

"Virginia, calm yourself. You'll become ill," Mr. Foster said gently. Then he left her and marched up the aisle to the recently abandoned desk. Flinging open the lid, he reached inside and lifted out the baby

33

snake. It writhed helplessly in the teacher's grasp. "I do not believe 'huge creature' accurately describes this tiny reptile, daughter."

At the sight of the snake, half a dozen girls leaped from their seats and began screaming. The boys doubled over with renewed laughter. Andi laughed right along with them. "I told you it would get better," she whispered to Rosa between giggles. But Rosa did not laugh.

Unexpectedly, Virginia crumpled onto the floor in a heap, striking her head on the edge of the teacher's desk.

"Virginia fainted!" Davy Cooper shouted above the clamor. The classroom grew still. Andi swallowed her laughter. All of a sudden, the situation didn't seem so funny.

Mr. Foster opened a window and gave the unwelcome visitor a toss. Then he crossed to where his daughter lay unconscious. "Wake up, Virginia." He patted her cheek. "The snake is gone." Virginia's eyes flew open. Mr. Foster helped her to her feet and led her back to her desk. "Sit down now. It's all over."

Virginia collapsed into her seat. "Please send for Mother. I'm ill. I feel faint."

"Oooh!" Patricia Newton squealed. "Your forehead. It's bleeding!"

Virginia's fingers flew to her head. The sight of her own blood sent her into another round of hysterical crying.

Mr. Foster drew a handkerchief from his vest pocket. "It's nothing more than a scratch, daughter. Take this." He pressed the cloth to Virginia's forehead and guided her shaking hand to hold it firmly in place. "Now, stop crying."

When Virginia's sobs had quieted to a muffled whimpering, the teacher returned to the front of the room. He picked up his ruler. "Who put the snake in my daughter's desk?"

No one spoke. No one moved.

Mr. Foster tapped his ruler lightly across his palm. "I want a name."

Andi's gaze was riveted on the ruler in Mr. Foster's hand. She'd heard stories from her brothers about teachers who hit their students for the smallest offense, but she never dreamed she'd see it for herself. Miss Hall had been the gentlest of souls. Her punishments never went beyond a trip to the corner or a note sent home. *I bet this is the last snake Cory ever brings to class.* Andi's throat tightened in sympathy for her friend.

"*That* girl knows."

Andi whirled on Virginia. She was pointing directly at her. "*What?*"

Virginia hiccupped and rubbed the tears from her eyes. "She was sitting in this desk before I was. She must have known about the snake." She hiccupped again. "Perhaps she put it there herself."

Andi shook her head vigorously. "No, sir. I didn't."

"Then who did?"

Andi said nothing. She was no tattletale. Mr. Foster would have to find the culprit without her help.

The teacher sighed. "Very well, then. Did you know the snake was in your desk?"

Andi squirmed uncomfortably. "Yes, sir. But in all the confusion of switching seats, I forgot about it." She took a deep breath. "It was just a little snake—nothing to get all fired up about."

The schoolmaster pointed at Virginia. "Do you call terrifying a new student with a cruel joke and then laughing over it nothing to get all fired up about?"

"No, sir. I'm sorry, sir." She turned to Virginia. "I'm sorry you got hurt, Virginia."

With her father's blood-smeared handkerchief on the desk beside her, Virginia buried her head in her arms and refused to look at Andi.

Mr. Foster picked up the list of rules and scanned them. "Miss Carter, the rules forbid bringing live creatures of any kind into this classroom." He looked up. "The punishment is four licks of the switch for boys, four licks of the ruler for girls." He dropped the paper and picked up his ruler. "Pass to the front."

Andi gulped. "I didn't bring the snake into class, Mr. Foster."

"Then who did?" When Andi made no reply, he motioned her forward.

By the time she reached Mr. Foster's desk, Andi was near panic. The teacher towered over her, his lips set in a firm, disapproving line. He reached out and took hold of her hand.

"Wait, Teacher!" A white-faced Cory sprang from his seat. "Andi's not to blame. I put the snake in her desk. She told me not to, but I did it anyway."

It's about time! Andi wanted to shout at Cory. She felt weak with relief.

"That's right," Jack added. "Cory's always one for bringin' in snakes an' spiders and things."

Mr. Foster appeared unmoved. "I'm afraid your confessions come too late, boys. Miss Carter's punishment will serve as a lesson to all of you that I am not a schoolmaster to be trifled with. Next time, speak up at once." He raised his ruler and brought it down against Andi's palm with a loud *whack*.

Blinking back tears of anger and humiliation, Andi returned to her seat in disgrace. The four licks didn't hurt nearly as much as the shame of being punished unjustly—especially on the first day of school.

"I'm sorry I waited to speak up," Cory apologized, leaning over Andi's shoulder. "I didn't think he'd punish you. Not the first day. Not with Justin on the school board. I botched things up pretty bad, but I'll make it up to you. I promise. Don't be sore for keeps."

Andi shrugged Cory's apology away. She could never stay mad at him for longer than a few minutes, no matter how hard she tried. But her anger with Mr. Foster was a different matter. She'd seen the gleam in his eyes just before he whacked her palm. She was certain he was using the snake incident as an excuse to punish her for nearly trampling him the other day. Why else would he be so ridiculously unfair?

She returned her attention to the front of the classroom when Mr. Foster began speaking. He held a large black Bible in his hands. "The board has decided that each school day will begin with a selection from the Holy Scriptures." He made a great show of leafing through the pages of the Bible. When he found the place, he cleared his throat and began reading, "'Blessed is the man that walketh not in the counsel of the ungodly, nor standeth in the way of sinners, nor . . .'"

Andi listened in disappointment as Mr. Foster droned his way through Psalm 1. He read the passage without feeling, as if it were nothing more than a dictionary entry. Andi knew the passage by heart, so she shut her ears to his voice and sent up a quick prayer that she could finish the rest of the day without any more clashes with the schoolmaster.

"Begin your lessons," Mr. Foster directed when he had finished. "I will place you into classes when I hear you recite."

Andi opened her reader and tried to concentrate on her lesson, but her thoughts kept returning to her earlier humiliation. A wave of longing for the familiar, cheerful confusion of Miss Hall's classroom rose up inside her. Miss Hall would never have asked who put the snake in the desk. She knew. She *always* knew. Cory would have been marched quickly to his usual corner without any fuss.

Andi moped. Right now she should be happily acquainting Rosa with the joys of learning to read and write. She'd looked forward to helping her friend adjust to a strange school and new customs. But now she felt trapped for seven hours a day in a classroom with a teacher whose word was law. He held an unfair grudge against her on account of her recklessness the other day, and he didn't appear willing to forgive her anytime soon.

To make matters worse, it looked like she'd ruined any chance of making friends with Virginia Foster. No doubt the girl's father would forbid his daughter to associate with such a brash and reckless girl as Andrea Carter. *He's probably afraid I'll run her over with my horse or torment her with another snake or something*, she thought gloomily.

She hazarded a peek at Virginia, who glanced back at the same time. Andi tried her best I'm-really-sorry-can-we-be-friends? smile, but Virginia wrinkled her pale eyebrows and pursed her thin lips into an expression that told Andi she was *not* interested.

Andi sighed. It was going to be a long term.

Chapter Five

THE ACCIDENT

The teacher knows you are in the tree," Rosa announced one noon recess two weeks later. She shaded her eyes and looked up, where Andi stood motionless on one of the ancient oak's huge, spreading branches. "Come down," she pleaded in her slow, careful English. "Please."

"In a minute," came Andi's breathless reply. "I've just about . . . got it!" she yelled triumphantly. "Here. Catch." She dropped a heavy canning jar into Rosa's waiting hands and quickly lowered herself to the ground. Immediately, a handful of excited little girls swarmed around her.

"It's so pretty!" seven-year-old Emily squealed as she threw her arms around Andi's waist. "I knew you could do it." She raised her head and gave Andi an adoring grin. "You can catch 'most anything, I bet—spiders, snakes, frogs, and the like."

Andi gently untangled the little girl's arms from around her waist. "Just about," she agreed with a smile. Then she bent down and whispered in her ear, "Would you like me to catch you a spider next time? I know where there's some 'specially big ones."

"No!" Emily shrieked. "I hate spiders." She reached for the jar in Rosa's hand, where a lovely orange and black monarch butterfly fluttered. She clutched her prize tightly to her chest. "Thank you!" Then she and her giggling little friends skipped away in a flurry of colorful skirts and pinafores.

Andi brushed leaves and twigs from her dress and looked up at the second-story window of the schoolhouse. The teacher stood behind the glass with his arms locked in front of his chest, frowning at her—as usual. She winced. Caught again!

"I'll be copying lines today," she grumbled to Rosa. "You just wait and see. I can't turn around without Mr. Foster punishing me for breaking some dumb rule of etiquette. He finds fault with everything I do. I think it's his way of reminding me that he hasn't forgotten about the trampling." She wrinkled her brow. "But what I can't figure out is how he catches me so often. He can't be everywhere at once. How did he happen to be at the window just as I was catching that butterfly?"

"I think he has help," Rosa said. "*Mira*—look."

Andi glanced up at the window. Her jaw tightened. Mr. Foster had disappeared from view, but the second-story classroom was by no means empty. Virginia stood at the window, all alone, watching the activity in the schoolyard.

Andi turned away from the window, suddenly uneasy. "You're right, Rosa. It looks like Virginia's running to her father with tales about me. I've tried a couple times to be nice to her, but she's not about to forget Cory's snake. And that wasn't even my fault." She shook her head. "This term's getting worse by the day."

Just then small, curly-haired Toby Wright raced up and yanked on Andi's sleeve, pulling her rudely from her conversation. "Hey! Why did you catch Emily a swell butterfly like that?"

"Three reasons," Andi replied, brushing his hand away. "First, she asked me to catch it. Second, she gave me the jar. And third . . ."—she jabbed a finger into the little boy's chest—"she won't stick it with a pin and mount it on a piece of wood. She'll let it go."

"What a waste of a good butterfly," Toby mumbled. Then he grinned up at Andi. "Cory sent me to fetch you to come play ball. Seth hurt his arm last inning, so Cory needs a new player."

"Can't he ask Ollie?"

Toby shook his head. "You know Ollie can't see good enough to hit the ball. Cory wants *you*. He says you play near as good as anybody on the team." He grabbed Andi's hand. "C'mon."

Andi turned to Rosa, who shrugged. "I think maybe you will be copying many, *many* lines if you do this," her friend predicted gloomily.

Andi paused in indecision. Playing baseball was nearly as much fun as racing her horse. Miss Hall had always tolerated her playing ball with the boys, and Andi had never given her former teacher any reason to withdraw the privilege. Mr. Foster would probably disapprove, but he was nowhere in sight. Neither was his daughter. The noon hour was just about over. What could it hurt? She shook off her uneasiness and hurried over to the dusty field behind the schoolhouse.

"Over here, Andi!" Cory motioned wildly. He grabbed her hand and pulled her into the clump of players waiting their turn to bat. "You're just in time. You're taking Seth's place, and you're up next."

"Batter up!" Jack Goodwin yelled impatiently from his position as catcher. "We haven't got all day."

Andi grabbed the bat and headed for the rough square of wood that served as home plate. She eyed the pitcher and scowled. Huge Johnny Wilson scowled back. He loosened the collar of his fancy Sunday shirt and kicked aside the expensive suit coat lying in a heap at his feet.

"No girls," he objected loudly, planting his meaty fists on his hips.

"What do you care?" Cory shot back. "She's not on your team."

Johnny glared at Andi for a moment, then shrugged. "Suit yourself. But I'm not going easy on her just 'cause she's a girl."

"Who's asking you to?" Andi shouted. "Play ball!"

Johnny's expression twisted into a sneer. With a sudden snap of his wrist, he hurled the ball toward home plate. Andi swung. The ball flew past her and landed in the catcher's bare hands with a loud smack.

"That's a strike," Jack said with a grimace. He tossed the ball back to the pitcher and rubbed his stinging palms against his britches.

Johnny caught the ball and snickered. "Too fast for you, Andi?" Before she could respond, he threw the ball a second time. Andi clenched her teeth and swung. The ball cracked against the bat and popped up, back over her head. It bounced a couple of times and rolled to a stop near the corner of the schoolhouse. Foul ball.

Jack grinned at her before going after the ball. "Cory's team's gonna lose if you go on hitting like that."

"Keep quiet," Andi muttered, swinging the bat to her shoulder.

Johnny caught the ball and smirked. He threw the next pitch.

Andi swung. The ball flew up and back over her head.

"Another foul," Jack grumbled. "I'm tired of chasing your—" He gasped. "Oh, no!"

Andi spun around just in time to watch the ball hit a second-story window of the schoolhouse. There was an earsplitting *CRACK* followed by the tinkling of a thousand pieces of glass. Then silence. All activity in the schoolyard ceased as each pupil turned his attention first to the smashed window, then to the ballplayers.

Andi dropped the bat and stared at the window in stunned disbelief. Her teammates crowded around her, eyes wide and scared.

Johnny broke the silence with a nervous laugh. "Great hit, Andi." He came and stood beside her. "Maybe next time you'll hit old Foster right on the head."

"Shut up, Johnny," Cory snapped.

The door to the schoolhouse flew open. The schoolmaster raced down the back steps, followed more slowly by a pale-faced Miss Hall.

"The classroom is a shambles!" Mr. Foster bellowed, coming to a stop in the middle of the field. His face was suffused with rage. "My daughter came close to being seriously injured. Who is responsible for this?"

No one answered. By now, every pupil, young and old, had been drawn to the ball field. Some of the smaller children were crying. When they saw Miss Hall, they ran to her and clutched her skirt.

Mr. Foster looked at the crying children and the bewildered Miss Hall, and composed himself. With a shaking hand, he pulled a handkerchief from his waistcoat pocket and mopped his forehead. "This doesn't concern any of your scholars, Miss Hall," he said at last. "The noon recess is over. Please take the younger ones inside."

The rest of the little children ran to Miss Hall like frightened chicks looking for their mother. She gathered them up and guided them into the schoolhouse, out of sight of the angry Mr. Foster.

The schoolmaster returned his attention to the boys, who now cowered together in a nervous clump. "Who broke the window?"

His question was met with utter silence. Most of the boys shuffled their feet and stared at the ground. Even Johnny Wilson looked uncomfortable. He slung his suit coat over his shoulder and studied the tops of his shoes.

Mr. Foster drew himself up. "If no one confesses, every boy here will be punished."

Andi's heart pounded against the inside of her chest like a mighty fist. She knew everyone expected her to speak up. If she didn't, the boys would all be punished, and it would be her fault. She swallowed and opened her mouth to speak, but no words came out.

"I did it." Cory's unexpected confession drew startled looks from the other boys. There were gasps from the watching girls, including Andi. Cory picked up the bat and handed it to Mr. Foster. "It was an accident. I'll clean it up right away." He turned to Andi, warning her with a look.

"Mr. Blake. I might have known." He grasped the boy's ear. Cory yelped. "Come along with me, boy. You will feel the switch today."

Andi groaned as Mr. Foster dragged Cory away. She wanted to run after the teacher and set things straight, but her legs felt like jelly.

"Cory's sure gonna get it," Davy Cooper remarked, kicking at a rock.

"Cory's a fool," Johnny said. He joined the small crowd making its way slowly back to the schoolhouse. "I wouldn't take the blame for no girl."

"You gonna tell the teacher?" Peter Kincaid wanted to know. He gave Andi a worried look.

Johnny shook his head. "Nope. If Cory wants to act all noble and take Andi's thrashing, I guess that's his business."

"None of us'll tell," Davy assured Andi. He spread his arms to include the dozen or so girls who had wandered over to watch. "One thrashing today is plenty." There were nods all around. "We'll all stick by you, Andi."

The loyalty of her friends should have cheered her, but it didn't. Instead, she felt miserable for not speaking up.

The students climbed the stairs in uneasy silence and entered the classroom in time to see the teacher administering the last of several well-aimed strokes to Cory's backside. Andi cringed at the sight and quickly found her seat.

"Now, clean up this mess, Mr. Blake."

"Yes, sir," Cory replied stiffly. He headed to the back of the room for a broom.

"The rest of you should check carefully for glass splinters before seating yourselves," Mr. Foster said. "Fourth Reader Class, gather your books and come forward for recitation." He frowned suddenly. "Yes? What is it, Miss Foster?"

Virginia stood beside her desk and curtsied. "Father, I think I need to tell you something."

"Does it concern your recitation?"

Virginia shook her head. "No, Father. It concerns the broken window." She took a deep breath. "The truth is, sir, Cory Blake did not break it."

Mr. Foster narrowed his eyes. "Are you certain?"

"Yes, sir. If you recall, I stayed indoors during the noon hour. I was watching the ball game from over there." She pointed to the far side of the classroom. "The ball crashed through the window not ten feet from where I was standing. Andrea Carter was holding the bat."

Mr. Foster turned a disbelieving look on Andi. "*You* broke the window?"

"I broke it," Cory insisted from the back of the room. "Ask anybody."

"Wait!" Andi jumped to her feet. Cory's lie would only dig the two of them into deeper trouble. It was time to make things right. "Virginia's right. I broke it. But it was an accident, just like Cory said." She swallowed the lump that had suddenly appeared. "I'm sorry, sir. I really am."

Mr. Foster turned to Virginia. "Thank you for speaking up." He called gruffly to Cory, "Mr. Blake, return to your seat. Miss Carter, you will clean up the glass. Then you will stay after class and write in your copybook one hundred times, *I will not deceive the teacher.*"

"I—I can't stay after class today," Andi stammered. "My brother needs to—"

"You *will* stay, Miss Carter. Is that understood?" When Andi nodded, he pointed to the remaining pieces of glass. "Now, find the broom and do as I ask."

The teacher's command propelled Andi toward the back of the room. As she passed Cory's desk, he handed her a hastily scribbled note. It read, "Sorry. I was trying to make up for the snake."

Cramming the note into her dress pocket, Andi glanced at Cory. He gave her an apologetic smile. She forced a smile in return. Then she grabbed the broom and finished cleaning up the mess.

Chapter Six

A ROTTEN AFTERNOON

Andi slammed her copybook shut and let out a weary sigh. For the past hour the only sound in the classroom had come from the *scratch, scratch, scratch* of pen against paper as she scribbled out one hundred of the longest sentences of her life. *I will not deceive the teacher* was burned into her mind, but the hot flush that raced through her fingers she wrote had nothing to do with shame or remorse over her behavior. Justin had promised to take her home right after school today. Now a whole hour of precious riding time was wasted! All because of . . .

"That snippety Virginia Foster," she murmured. She capped the ink jar, cleaned her pen tip, and placed the pen in her desk. "Why couldn't she keep her mouth shut? Or at least tell her father who broke the window *before* he whipped Cory?"

Hoping Mr. Foster hadn't heard her critical remark about his daughter, she glanced up and found the classroom deserted. Quickly, she gathered her books and rose from her desk. She wasn't sure why the schoolmaster had stepped out, but she decided she wasn't going to stick around and wait for his return. She'd already spent more time in town this afternoon than she liked.

The heat of her anger had dropped only a few degrees by the time she clattered down the stairs and burst through the double doors into the bright afternoon sun. Perhaps a brisk ride home would help her sort out her feelings. Maybe Justin would let her drive the buggy or—

Andi stopped short. Right in front of the schoolhouse, her brother

46

stood next to the buggy, passing the time with Mr. Foster. The sight of the men speaking together cooled Andi off faster than a bucket of cold water.

"Well, well, the prodigal returns," Justin called out when he saw her. He smiled and waved her over.

Andi pasted a smile on her face and joined them. "I'm finished, Mr. Foster," she forced herself to say. "May I go now?"

Mr. Foster regarded her silently for a moment. Then he nodded. "I hope this exercise has been an incentive to help curb your . . . *exuberance*," he said, unsmiling. "Has it?"

"Yes, sir."

He gave her a doubtful look and turned to Justin. "Your sister is rather high-spirited," he remarked in a disapproving voice, "and a touch reckless, I'm afraid."

"Really?" Justin replied, raising his eyebrows. He looked ready to laugh. Andi wanted to kick him for amusing himself at her expense.

"Yes, Mr. Carter. But with the proper guidance, it may be possible to bring her under control before it is too late."

"No doubt," Justin agreed quickly. "Now if you'll excuse us, it's a long drive back to the ranch."

"Of course." Mr. Foster shook Justin's hand, touched the brim of his hat to Andi, and turned to leave. "Good day, Mr. Carter. Tell your mother I'm looking forward to Saturday," were his parting words.

Andi stared at Mr. Foster's retreating form until Justin's voice brought her around. "Do you plan on standing here all afternoon, or would you like a ride home?" He smiled and reached out a helping hand.

Andi grasped her brother's hand and swung herself effortlessly into the rig. "Where's Rosa?"

Justin climbed up beside her. "Rosa got tired of waiting. She saw her father in town picking up supplies for Chad and caught a ride back to the ranch."

"I suppose you got tired of waiting, too."

"Yes, I did." Justin gave the horse a chirrup, and they started down the street. "That's why I came looking for you."

"Didn't Rosa tell you what happened?"

"No. But Mr. Foster did."

Silence.

Justin flicked the reins across Pal's back. "May I look at the sentences?"

Andi felt a warm flush creep into her cheeks as she pulled out her copybook and opened it to four pages of small, neat script.

Justin took the book with his free hand and skimmed the pages. "Would you care to explain to me why you lied to your teacher?"

No, I wouldn't care to explain, Andi wanted to say. But she took a deep breath and plunged into the whole awful story. It didn't take long to tell.

"That's pretty much the same story I heard from Mr. Foster," Justin remarked with a sigh. He slammed the copybook shut and dropped it in her lap. "However, his retelling was sprinkled with several unflattering comments about your behavior in his classroom."

"I didn't mean to deceive him, Justin. I tried to tell him, but I was so scared. The words got stuck. Then Cory jumped in and . . . well, you know the rest."

"I know you got yourself into another fix by not speaking up when you should have. Mr. Foster is strict, but I think this punishment is fair. We'll work out a way you can pay for the window, and that will be the end of it."

"It *won't* be the end of it! Mr. Foster's always riding me for anything he thinks might be the least bit improper for a young lady." She grimaced. "And your being on the school board doesn't help."

"Actually, I think your troubles began a couple of weeks ago. Nearly trampling your teacher wasn't the best way to begin the term, but I'm sure Mr. Foster will eventually put it behind him. After all, he did drop the charges."

"Only because I'm your sister."

Justin chuckled. "See? I'm good for something." He pulled Andi into a quick hug. "Once Mr. Foster becomes comfortable with his pupils, and the older boys figure out who's in charge, I think he'll turn out to be a good schoolmaster. Just do me a favor and try to stay out of trouble. And be patient."

Be patient? Andi realized patience was not one of her strong points. She knew Justin knew it, too. That's why he was smiling.

"I'll try, Justin. I really will," she promised fervently.

"Good." He slapped the reins, and the large bay horse, which had slowed to a lazy walk during the conversation, broke into a trot.

Andi rode in silence for a few miles, mourning the fact that everything was going wrong on what should have been a perfect afternoon. The late summer sun had turned from scorching hot to pleasantly warm the past few days—perfect for a good, fast ride on her horse. Her mother had promised Andi that she would have time to ride if she came right home.

She scowled. Most of her free time today had been taken up writing sentences. When she arrived home, she'd have to confess to her mother about the broken window. When she did, she'd probably find herself with half a dozen unpleasant chores to pay for it. Worse, her favorite brother—while not exactly angry—didn't seem sympathetic to her problems. Worst of all, dumb old Virginia Foster was—

"Justin!" Andi jerked up from where she had been slouched against the seat, idly watching the scenery go by.

"What is it?" Justin asked, turning the buggy into the wide lane leading up to the ranch house.

"Remember back in town? You were talking with Mr. Foster about Saturday." She took a deep breath. "What's happening on Saturday?"

"We're having the new schoolmaster and his family out to the ranch for supper. A welcoming meal and some friendly conversation."

Andi stared at her brother in disbelief. "The entire family? Virginia, too?"

"Of course."

"This is terrible! Mother will expect me to entertain Virginia."

"Probably. Why shouldn't you entertain her for an afternoon?"

"Because whenever I'm with Virginia, something dreadful happens. You don't know her like I do."

Justin slowed the horse to a walk. "You can't know her very well. School's been in session barely two weeks."

"I know her well enough to figure out that we're never going to be friends. She's—she's . . . well, she's prissy and snippety and . . . and . . ." She slumped against the seat. This conversation was not going well. "And she can't take a joke. She blamed *me* for Cory's snake being in her desk, even though it wasn't my fault. She thinks I'm some kind of rowdy tomboy, and—"

"And she probably holds it against you for nearly killing her father."

"That, too," Andi agreed with a heavy heart. "So you see, I simply *cannot* entertain her on Saturday. She doesn't like me at all." She gave her brother a pleading look. "You understand, don't you?"

Justin broke into a wide, teasing grin. "Perfectly. But I doubt Mother will."

Andi groaned. Justin was right, as usual. Her mother would not understand. Even if she did sympathize, it wouldn't make the slightest difference. She'd expect Andi to set aside her own feelings and entertain Virginia Foster for as long as the family stayed. Showing hospitality—whether one liked the guests or even *knew* them—was an unspoken rule on the Circle C Ranch.

"Will you talk to Mother, Justin? This once? I promise I'll—"

"I'm afraid this is one area over which I have no influence. Even Father bowed to Mother's wishes when it comes to entertaining guests. If you knew how often Chad and I got our backsides tanned

ANDREA CARTER AND THE DANGEROUS DECISION

for misbehaving when unwelcome guests came calling . . ." A smile pulled at the corners of his mouth.

"Tell me, Justin!"

"The time I remember best was when Chad stuffed Freddy Stone's foul mouth full of dirt and tossed him into the horse trough." He chuckled at the memory. "Freddy was one of those annoying little boys who dressed like a sissy and behaved perfectly around the adults, but he played dirty tricks on the other kids. Chad decided a whipping was a fair price to pay for entertaining Freddy in a way he'd never forget."

"I bet it was something," Andi remarked in delight. Perhaps she was talking to the wrong brother. Maybe Chad would sympathize enough to offer her a workable solution.

"I'm sure things will go fine on Saturday," Justin said, "so long as you're not tempted to toss Virginia into the horse trough."

"That's not funny, big brother."

Justin was still chuckling when they drove through the gate and into the yard. He pulled the horse to a stop and gave an appreciative whistle. "Take a look at that, honey." Right in front of them, prancing around the corral, was a magnificent dappled gray horse.

Andi caught her breath and nearly fell from the buggy in her hurry to see the horse. "They got him, Justin! They finally caught Whirlwind," she called over her shoulder. Then she took off running toward the corral.

Before she had gone a dozen steps, a pair of strong hands grabbed her around the waist and swung her around. "Whoa there, little sister." Chad's voice carried a hint of warning. "Where d'you think you're headed?"

"Oh, Chad! You got him. Can't I see him up close?" She tried to wriggle free from her brother's grasp, but he held on tight and shook his head.

"Not yet. He's too spooked. It'll be awhile before anyone goes

51

near him. I want you, especially, to stay away from him. Do you hear me?"

"But . . ."

"No, Andi."

Andi settled down reluctantly and watched the beautiful horse run around the corral. She'd almost lost her life last spring because of her disobedience in going near one of her brother's wild stallions. Perhaps Chad knew best, after all.

"He's a beauty." She turned around. "Where did you catch him?"

"Up in the hills." Chad looked mighty pleased with himself. He crossed his arms and watched the horse with satisfaction. "It took a couple of weeks, but we finally caught up with him and his band this morning. Got the mares back, too."

"What're you going to do with him?"

"Break him—I hope. Then sell him. He's good horseflesh, even with that wild streak." He grinned suddenly. "You want to help?"

Andi looked up into her brother's bright blue eyes and gasped. Was he teasing her? "Me? You mean it?"

"I sure do," he said. "Just give me a couple of weeks with him first. I'll be able to judge him better after that. If it looks like he's going to behave himself, I'll let you help with some of the gentling. I can't promise more than that, and I don't know what Mother will say to any of it."

Andi threw her arms around her brother's waist and gave him a grateful hug. "You don't have to worry about what Mother'll say. She always lets you make decisions about the ranch."

"Just make sure you keep your end of the bargain," Chad warned her. "Right now that animal's dangerous. Don't let your curiosity get the better of you."

"I won't. I'll do anything you say."

"Good. How about starting on your chores?"

Andi's joy vanished. "Oh. Yeah. Chores." She made no move to begin.

Chad took her firmly by the shoulders and spun her around in the direction of the horse barn. "The chores are that way. Feed the horses and make sure you check their water. It's been pretty hot lately. When you're finished, you can straighten up your tack. You've got bridles and brushes and your saddle and blanket scattered from one end of the barn to the other. We have a tack room, you know."

"I know." Andi shrugged away from her brother's hold, crossed the yard, and entered the barn. "Taffy! I'm home." She glanced around the dim interior, hoping her brother Mitch might be nearby. Twice this week he'd helped her with her chores. Maybe he would do them again today so she could ride Taffy longer.

She heard a scraping sound, and a large shadow filled the doorway, blocking the afternoon sun. With a grin, Andi spun around, all set to charm Mitch into giving her some help. Her smile faded when she recognized Chad leaning against the doorpost.

"Expecting somebody else?" he drawled, lip twitching. Before Andi could reply, he continued, "If you think you can sweet-talk Mitch into doing your chores again today, it's too late. I sent him on a cattle-buying trip. He won't be home 'til Friday."

Andi snatched up a hoof pick and hurled it at her brother, furious that he could so easily figure out what she was thinking. Chad caught the pick out of the air and dropped it carelessly onto a bale of hay. Then he turned and left the barn, chuckling softly.

Andi ripped apart the dry, sweet-smelling alfalfa hay and began pitching it to the hungry horses in their stalls. When she reached her own horse's stall, she paused. "I tell you, Taffy, I've had one miserable day. What do you say I finish up here in a hurry, and we go for a ride?" Taffy snorted her agreement and tossed her head. Andi gave the mare a friendly pat and whispered, "*Then* I'll tell Mother about the broken window."

Chapter Seven

An Afternoon with Virginia

Andi lay across her sister's bed in gloomy silence and watched seventeen-year-old Melinda brush out her beautiful golden hair. She arranged it in a complicated style and turned away from the mirror. Her hands held up heavy lengths of blond ringlets. "So," she mumbled through lips crammed full of hairpins, "what do you think?" A pin dropped to the floor as she spoke.

Andi cocked her head and regarded her sister carefully. "I don't think you'll be able to eat very well, holding your hair up like that."

Melinda's expression twisted in annoyance. She opened her mouth, and the rest of the hairpins fell to the floor. "Andrea Carter, you know good and well what I meant." She dropped her hands to her sides with an exasperated sigh. Her golden hair tumbled past her shoulders in wild disarray.

Andi sat up. "I don't know why you're fixing your hair all fancy and dressing up. You won't be able to take a decent breath after you lace that corset up tight." She shuddered at the thought of sacrificing comfort for fashion. "It's only the Fosters coming for supper—not Jeffery Sullivan."

Melinda reached down and began collecting hairpins from the floor. "Just because we live on a ranch doesn't mean we can't look and act like ladies. Grace is acquainted with all the latest hairstyles and fashions, and she's bringing the new *Godey's Lady's Book* to go through. I want to look nice for our guests."

Andi dropped to the floor next to her sister and scooped up the rest of the hairpins. She handed them over with a smile. "Melinda, I think your hair looks beautiful—like always. You're the nicest, prettiest sister in the whole world. I know Virginia would love to look at fashion plates and talk about the latest Eastern styles and read poems and stories in *Godey's*. You'll let her join you, won't you?"

"Sorry, Andi, but Grace and I have already made our plans." Melinda returned to her seat, picked up a brush, and began vigorously attacking her hair.

Andi plopped back onto the bed. "Aw, c'mon. If you entertain Virginia along with her sister, I'll do whatever you ask for a whole week. I'll make your bed, clean your room, brush your horse . . ." She took a deep breath. "I'll even be nice to Jeffrey Sullivan when he comes calling tomorrow after church. Please, Melinda. I *can't* spend an afternoon with Virginia." Her sister was her last hope. She'd gotten absolutely nowhere with her brothers.

Melinda jabbed a hairpin into a stubborn lock of gold. "Honestly, Andi, she can't be as bad as you say. Grace is delightful. Why don't you show Virginia your horse? Maybe you two can go riding."

"Ha!" Andi scoffed. "I bet Virginia doesn't even know which end of the horse to bridle."

"Andi!" Melinda exclaimed. "That was unkind."

"I'm sorry, but I don't like her at all. Nobody else does, either. She acts prissy and ladylike in front of her father, but she's a different person when he's not around—sneaky and bossy. And another thing, she's always showing off how smart she is."

"You better not let Mother hear you talking like that," Melinda warned. "Virginia's our guest, and it's your responsibility to amuse her this afternoon."

"So everyone keeps telling me," Andi said with a pout. "How am I supposed to do that?"

A new voice broke in. "By conducting yourself like a Christian young lady and remembering your duty as a hostess." Elizabeth Carter glided into the bedroom with a smile for her daughters. "I realize Virginia and you might not have much in common, Andrea. I'm not asking you to make her your best friend—just treat her with courtesy and kindness. Remember? Do unto others . . . ?"

"I know, I know," Andi said. "As I would have others do unto me." She let out a breath. She'd heard *that* plenty of times before—and she usually tried to remember it. But with Virginia? "Couldn't I stay in my room this afternoon? Just tell the Fosters I'm ill." She laid a hand over her stomach and winced. "I really don't feel very well. . . ." Her voice trailed away at her mother's shaking head.

"You can't hide from people you don't like," Elizabeth said, joining Andi on the bed. "Part of growing up means learning to get along with folks—especially those who rub you the wrong way. I'm sure if you look beyond Virginia's shortcomings, you'll find something pleasant to talk about."

"Like what?"

"Well . . . the Fosters just moved here from back East. You could ask her how she likes the West. I also know they visited Yosemite just before school started. You could let her talk about her trip. Perhaps if you show an interest in some of the things she's seen or done, she'll warm up."

Andi sighed. "Mother, she thinks I'm a tomboy. She doesn't want anything to do with me."

"Then why don't you show her another side—the polite and well-mannered daughter I've tried to raise? Show a little compassion to a newcomer, Andrea. Virginia has been uprooted, moved from everything familiar, and set down in the middle of a small, dusty town. She's probably feeling frightened and insecure, unsure how to act around the other girls." Elizabeth smiled suddenly. "How would you like it if I were teaching in your classroom every day?"

Andi made a face. "I wouldn't like it."

"No, you wouldn't. Put yourself in Virginia's place. Her father is the schoolmaster. From what Justin tells me, the man has high standards of excellence for both academics and behavior. Imagine having to be the teacher's daughter with those kinds of expectations." Andi grimaced. She'd had firsthand experience with Mr. Foster's strict demands. She couldn't imagine the man as her *father*! A sudden twinge of compassion for Virginia stirred her heart.

Elizabeth stood up and laid her hands gently on Andi's shoulders. "I know I can count on you to treat Virginia as an honored guest, in spite of the way you feel about her."

"I'll try, Mother. But it won't be easy."

"I never said it would be easy. Perhaps a quick prayer while you're changing your clothes will help keep you in the right frame of mind. Now, run along. It's nearly time for our guests to arrive."

Andi trudged to her room, pulled off her everyday clothes, and struggled into a pale green frock with just enough ruffles and lace to get in her way. She pulled out her braids and ran a brush through tangles of unruly dark waves that fell to her waist. As usual, her hair had a mind of its own. It wouldn't stay tied up behind the bow, and loose curls fell into her eyes. Impatiently, she pushed them back.

Andi looked at her reflection. "This is going to be a long afternoon," she whispered to the girl staring back at her. She raised her gaze to the ceiling. "All I ask is that you help me keep my temper, Lord." Then she forced her features into a pleasant expression. "Talk about Yosemite, huh? I guess I could give it a try."

Andi left her room and headed for the stairs, where she met Rosa, dust cloth in hand. "I wish I was dusting the second floor today and *you* were amusing Virginia," she remarked wistfully.

Rosa's cloth swirled along the banister railing. "Days like these make me glad that I am the hired girl. I would not trade places with you for all the gold in California."

Andi couldn't blame her. She eyed the railing, weighed the

consequences of sliding in her Sunday frock, and wisely chose to walk down the stairs.

The afternoon started off pleasantly enough. There were polite greetings all around. Melinda and the older Foster girl headed for the library, where they could talk and giggle in private. Andi greeted Virginia and offered to take her up to her room.

"No." Virginia brushed aside a pale wisp of hair and smoothed down her skirt. "I want to see the ranch."

Andi threw her a suspicious look.

"Now, Virginia," Mrs. Foster began, encircling her slender daughter in her arms. "You know you're not used to the climate yet. It's unbearably hot outside, and the dust will dirty your clothes. Perhaps you should stay inside with the others." She looked at her hostess. "Later, Virginia has a musical piece to share. She plays piano so well."

"That will be lovely," Elizabeth agreed.

"Do you play piano, Andrea?" Mrs. Foster asked.

Andi grinned. "No, ma'am. But I ride pretty well."

It was the wrong thing to say, Andi realized in a flash. Any mention of horseback riding was sure to bring back dreadful memories for the Fosters.

"Perhaps you'd like to practice your piece, Virginia?" Elizabeth put in smoothly. "Andrea would be happy to listen."

Andi straightened up at her mother's intense gaze. "I sure would," she said quickly. "Come on, Virginia. I'll show you to the—"

"No." Virginia's dark eyes filled with tears. "I want to go outdoors. Please, Mama. You never let me do anything. I really want to see the ranch. *Please.*"

Mrs. Foster turned to Elizabeth. "Is the ranch safe?"

"The Circle C is no more dangerous than the streets of Fresno. In some ways, safer," Elizabeth assured her guest with a smile. "Andrea will see to Virginia's welfare. She knows the ranch well."

"All right, then," Mrs. Foster conceded with a little sigh. "But keep your sunbonnet on, Virginia. Your skin cannot take this harsh western sun."

"Yes, Mama," Virginia chirped happily, pulling the strings to her bonnet forward. "Come on, Andrea. Let's go."

Andi didn't move. She had no wish to be responsible for Virginia's safety. "I think I'd rather stay inside, Mother."

It was no use. Her mother flashed her a be-a-good-little-hostess look and handed Andi her hat. "Have a lovely time, girls." She opened the door.

Andi plopped her black felt hat onto her head and followed Virginia out of the house.

"You look silly," Virginia giggled when they were alone. "That old hat with your party dress."

"It keeps the sun off, same as your bonnet. Now, what do you want to see?"

Virginia rolled her eyes. "I only wanted to go outdoors to be rid of my mother. She hovers over me all the time." She sighed. "Mothers can be such a trial, don't you agree?"

Andi didn't agree, but it wouldn't do any good to say it aloud. "Do you want to go riding?" she asked, hoping the afternoon wouldn't be a complete waste.

For an instant, Virginia's eyes lit up. Then she shook her head and smoothed down her skirt. "Heavens, no! I'd soil my dress. If I'd known you wanted to ride, I would have worn my habit."

Andi looked at Virginia in surprise. "Really? Well, maybe another time you and I could—"

A gasp from Virginia cut Andi off. "What a magnificent animal." Eyes wide, she pointed in the direction of the corral. Chad's rogue stallion paced back and forth along the inside of the fence. His mane and tail shimmered. He whinnied at the sight of the girls. "What's his name?"

Andi felt her spirits rise. She was always eager to talk about horses—even to Virginia. Perhaps they could be friends after all. "His name's Whirlwind. Isn't he a beauty? Chad's breaking him, and . . ." she couldn't help adding a bit smugly, "he's letting me help."

Virginia seemed astonished. "Why would he let you do that? Isn't he afraid you'll be hurt?"

Andi shook her head. "Chad knows what he's doing."

Virginia watched Whirlwind circle the corral. Her face showed her longing. "When will he be ready to ride?"

"Not for a long, long time. Why?"

Virginia shaded her eyes and squinted toward the corral. "My father promised Gracie and me a horse if we moved West." Her brow furrowed. "Perhaps I'll tell him we want this one."

"You can't ride Whirlwind." Andi wasn't even sure Chad would let *her* ride him.

Virginia narrowed her dark eyes. "Do you think I can't ride a horse?"

Andi didn't know *what* to think. "Whirlwind is not the horse for you or your sister. But we've got some nice—"

"Oh, and you think you know which horse is good for us?"

"I didn't mean to make you mad," Andi said. "I only meant—"

"I think I'd like to go riding, after all," Virginia broke in. She lifted her skirts and began hurrying toward the horse barn.

Andi scurried to catch up. "We have to go inside and change first."

Virginia stopped. "Whatever for?"

"I didn't think you wanted to spoil your clothes. I have riding clothes you can borrow."

A shadow fell across Virginia's face, and she shook her head. "If I go in the house, Mama will insist I rest or read or practice my piece." She set her jaw. "I'm—I'm going riding."

Andi heard the hesitation in Virginia's voice. "You *can* ride, can't you?" she asked.

"Of course." Virginia started walking. "Besides, even if I couldn't, how hard can it be to sit on a horse's back and hang on?"

The two girls entered the barn, where Andi soon discovered she had two horses to get ready. Virginia didn't lift a finger to help, and acted hurt when Andi suggested it. "I don't want to soil my dress," she gave as her excuse.

Andi bit her tongue to keep from reminding her guest how dirty she was likely to get just from riding. Did she think saddles were boiled to keep them clean? Or that the dust would stay where Virginia commanded it? Or that she was changing her excuses as fast as a chameleon changes colors?

Once outside, she watched and waited while Virginia tentatively patted Pal in all the wrong places, circled him twice, and examined each part of the bridle and saddle with exasperating care.

"Are you going to mount up anytime soon?" Andi leaned carelessly against Taffy and grinned. "It's not hard. You put your left foot in the stirrup, grab the saddle horn, and hike yourself up. Like this." With speed and grace from years of practice, Andi mounted Taffy. Then she jumped down and brushed off her skirt.

Virginia pouted. "You act like you don't believe I can ride."

"Can you?"

"I said I could!" She reached hesitant fingers toward the stirrup, shot an annoyed look in Andi's direction, and guided her foot into place. Closing her eyes, she curled her hand around the saddle horn. Then she took a deep breath and eased herself off the ground.

Pal shied away.

Virginia shrieked and nearly tumbled to the ground. Quickly, Andi lent a helping hand to Virginia's backside and boosted her into the saddle. The girl's face was pasty, and Andi couldn't help but notice how tightly she was clutching the saddle horn.

"Virginia . . ." she began, suddenly uneasy. What if her guest was all talk? What if she couldn't ride after all? "You'd better let me mount up behind you. We can ride double for a while."

"Nonsense! I'll show *you*, Andrea Carter, that it's no great trick to ride a horse." She raised her heels in the air.

"No, Virginia! Don't kick him!" Andi snatched at the bridle.

Too late. Virginia drove her heels into Pal's flank. The startled horse snorted his surprise and took off at a full gallop across the yard.

Chapter Eight

An Encounter with a Whirlwind

Andi groaned. She leaped onto Taffy and started after her blundering guest. "Pull back on the reins!" she yelled, before realizing Virginia didn't have the reins. They were flapping wildly around Pal's neck and head.

Virginia shrieked—long and loud. Andi could hear her terror as she raced to catch up. Poor Pal was trying to run away from the screaming nuisance on his back. "Hang on!" Andi shouted. "And stop yelling!"

Virginia was screaming too loudly to hear. Then suddenly, miraculously, one of the reins flew up where Virginia could snatch it from the air. She yanked on it, and Pal turned abruptly and raced back toward the corrals and outbuildings. The two of them hurtled past Andi, who pulled Taffy around and continued the chase. Grudging admiration and relief swept through her. It appeared that Virginia was not about to get herself dumped.

But Andi's relief was short-lived. Looming in front of the riders was the corral where Whirlwind pranced and whinnied, clearly agitated at seeing the other horses running wildly in the yard. Andi watched in horror as Pal rushed headlong toward the corral, guided by Virginia's one-handed grip on the reins.

Then it was over. Pal came to a bone-jarring stop at the corral fence. Wailing, Virginia went flying over the fence and crumpled to the ground with a dull thud. Her cries ceased instantly.

"Virginia!" Andi's heart pounded as she slid from Taffy's back and rushed to the corral. "Say something! Are you all right?" There was no answer. She squeezed between the railings, heedless of the ripping sound as her skirt caught and tore. Then she knelt beside Virginia and shook her. "Please be all right," she pleaded.

Her attention was diverted by a flash of gray and the thundering of hooves. Whirlwind tore past, took a mighty leap, and sailed effortlessly over the corral gate. Then he kicked up his hooves and made a mad dash for freedom, leaving a billowing cloud of dust behind.

"Oh, no!" Andi closed her eyes in dismay. "Chad's gonna skin me for sure."

With a groan, Virginia sat up and looked around. "Where am I?" she whispered in a shaking voice. Then her eyes widened. "Oh! That horse! That wild beast! He threw me." She gaped at Pal, who stood quietly on the other side of the fence.

"He stopped, and you kept going," Andi replied wearily. She was too drained to feel anything but relief that Virginia wasn't hurt. "You lied about being able to ride, didn't you?"

"You gave me a wild horse to ride," Virginia accused her. Then she noticed her dress. "Look at my dress. It's so full of dirt it will never come clean."

Andi frowned and rose to her feet. She offered Virginia her hand. "Never mind about your dumb dress. Just be thankful you're alive. Now, let's get out of here."

Trembling slightly, Virginia grasped Andi's hand and struggled to stand. "Ooh! My head hurts."

A sudden yell drew the girls' attention to the house. Andi watched a ranch hand gallop up, dismount, and bang frantically on the main door. "Boss! We got trouble." The door opened, and he disappeared inside.

A moment later, the door flew open, and Andi's three brothers raced toward the corral. The rest of the family and their guests hurried after them. They came to an abrupt halt when they saw the two disheveled girls standing in the empty corral.

Chad, as usual, reacted first. He slammed his palm against the railing of the deserted corral and glared at his sister. "Get yourself out of there—right now."

Andi jumped to obey. She yanked on Virginia's hand and hurried out of the enclosure.

Virginia broke into a loud wail and stumbled into her mother's arms. "Oh, Mama, I've never been so frightened in my life. I could have been killed."

Mr. Foster joined his wife and daughter. "What happened?"

"We were going riding," Andi began, "and Pal got away from—"

"Riding!" Mr. Foster's face paled. "Virginia doesn't ride."

"She tricked me into riding a wild beast of a horse," Virginia said. She looked at her father. "I didn't want to, but she made me. She promised it wouldn't hurt me. I told her I can't ride, but she just boosted me into the saddle and slapped that nasty horse on the rump. He ran away with me and threw me, and . . . and . . ." Virginia gulped. "Take me home, Mama."

"Virginia!" Andi gasped. "How can you tell such a dreadful lie?"

Mrs. Foster turned to Elizabeth. "Mrs. Carter, I—I scarcely know what to say. First my husband is nearly run over by these brutish western horses, and now my daughter has a similar experience." She gave Pal a fierce look. "It's a miracle Virginia didn't break her neck."

"It's her own fault," Andi insisted, clenching her fists. "Why won't anyone listen to me?"

"Andrea," Elizabeth warned with a frown. Then she turned to the Fosters. "Let's settle Virginia in the parlor with a cool drink. I'm sure she'll feel much better by the time supper is served."

"I'm afraid we must decline your offer, Mrs. Carter," Mr. Foster said. "I would like to take Virginia home. Besides, I fear I've lost my appetite." He turned to his wife and daughters. "Come, Margaret, Grace. We're leaving."

With a stiff good-bye to Elizabeth, the Fosters hurried away. Mr.

Foster helped his family settle into the large black surrey and turned for a final word. "I do not mean to sound presumptuous, Mrs. Carter, but let me suggest that what your wild girl needs is a serious thrashing. Perhaps that might curb her independent and reckless spirit." He took his place in the surrey, flicked the reins, and drove away.

Andi bit her tongue to keep from crying out at Mr. Foster's cruel words. Blinking back tears of rage and shame, she watched the surrey disappear down the road. She knew she should try and explain this disaster to her mother, but her throat tightened up.

Nobody spoke. It was as if an enormous black cloud had suddenly settled over the ranch, dampening everyone's mood. Andi could feel the tension in the air. She knew Chad, especially, must be sore. The time and effort he'd spent in capturing Whirlwind had just gone to waste—all because of one silly, stupid girl. "I'm sorry the stallion got out, Chad," she said, "but—"

"I trusted you, Andi," Chad stormed, cutting her off. "I thought we had an agreement." He threw up his hands. "It took us weeks to capture that animal. He'll waste no time rounding up those mares again, and we'll be right back where we started. Not to mention how *dangerous*—"

"It wasn't my fault!" Andi yelled. "I didn't go near him. Honest, I didn't. Whirlwind got spooked when Virginia landed in the corral."

"I don't care whose fault it is. You were in the corral. Now the horse is gone."

"Is this really necessary?" their mother broke in. "Granted, the stallion's escape is an annoyance, but the important thing is that no one was injured. Shouting at each other will not round up that horse."

Chad sighed. "You're right, Mother. I'll round up some of the men and see if we can track the stallion down." He gave Andi a disgusted look, then turned on his heel and headed for the bunkhouse.

"Now, Andrea," her mother said when Chad was out of sight. "What really happened?"

Andi took a deep breath. "Virginia lied about knowing how to ride. Pal took off with her. I was so scared. I went after her on Taffy, but . . . but . . . it was too late. She didn't know how to control him. When Pal stopped, Virginia went head over heels into the corral. Before I knew what was happening, Whirlwind raced past us and jumped the fence." She gave her mother a tiny smile. "You should've seen him, Mother. He was beautiful, flying over that fence." Then she lost her smile. Whirlwind was gone. Even if Chad managed to round him up again, she doubted he'd let her have anything to do with gentling him. Not now. Not after this disaster.

Her mother put an arm around her. "I believe you, sweetheart, and I'm sorry Mr. Foster spoke as he did. Let's remember that he was probably frightened at what happened to his daughter." She gave Andi a hug. "It's a mercy that Virginia escaped with no more than a good scare and maybe a few bruises. Losing the stallion pales next to what could have happened."

"Yes, ma'am," Andi whispered. She was very thankful Virginia was still in one piece. But still . . . "What about Chad? He's awful sore."

Justin glanced toward the bunkhouse. "Soon as the stallion's rounded up, Chad'll simmer down. But if you like, I'll go talk to him."

Andi nodded gratefully. Justin always knew what to say.

Mitch gave one of his sister's dark curls an affectionate tug. "Think I'll give Chad a hand with that stallion. It'll give him somebody else to yell at for a while." He headed after Justin.

Melinda grasped Andi's hand and gave it a friendly squeeze. "I'll take care of Taffy and Pal. You go with Mother and wash up."

Andi smiled at her sister. "Thanks, Melinda."

As she shuffled back to the house, Andi realized that the afternoon had gone exactly as she'd warned Justin it would, but it gave her no satisfaction to know she'd been right. Virginia had disrupted her life. She was the cause of a quarrel between Andi and her brother. She had proved to be the biggest liar west of the Sierras, and she'd managed to wheedle her way out of any blame. Instead, she had been petted and comforted with soft words. Worst of all, Mr. Foster had called Andi wild and reckless. Perhaps it was true—a little—but he needn't have said it out loud.

Andi threw herself onto her bed and buried her head in her pillow. *Oh, Lord,* she prayed, *I can't get along with Virginia, and I don't even want to try anymore. She's mean and spiteful. Surely you don't expect me to forgive her for this? I can't!*

She was still stewing when a quiet knock sounded at her door, and her mother called her to supper.

Chapter Nine

ANDI LOSES HER TEMPER

¿*Q*ué te pasa?"
      Andi looked up from where she sat on the front steps of the schoolhouse. Rosa was watching her with concern. "Nothing's the matter with me. I just want to sit here." She frowned and went back to watching the students run around the schoolyard. "You're not supposed to be speaking Spanish," she added with a grunt.

"You are still upset about Saturday," Rosa said matter-of-factly. She settled herself next to her friend, opened her lunch-pail, and took out a cold tamale. "Want this? It's your favorite. You know my mother makes the best tamales in the Valley."

A small smile replaced Andi's frown, but she shook her head. "I'm not hungry."

"You should forget this thing," Rosa said. She carefully unwrapped her meat-filled tamale from its cornhusk covering and took a large bite. "*Señor* Chad got his horse back, *no?*" she asked between mouthfuls.

Andi nodded. "Last night—finally."

"Now your brother is not so angry, right?"

"Wrong. Justin tried to smooth things over, but Chad's tired and grouchy. He didn't say more than two words to me at breakfast this morning." She drew a deep breath. "I know Luisa's upset, and your mother is, too, seeing that their special company dinner was only picked at. Nobody felt much like eating."

"I ate it," Rosa said cheerfully. "So did *Papá* and Joselito. *Mamá* also gave some to the ranch hands." She forced part of the tamale into Andi's hand. "Here. Eat." She unwrapped another tamale and continued. "What did the *señora* say about all this?"

Andi took a bite of the tamale. She chewed quietly for a moment. "We had a long talk Saturday evening. Actually, Mother did most of the talking. I was too busy bawling. She said I had to learn to get along with Virginia, no matter how I felt, and that meant forgiving her for lying."

"*¡Ay, no!*" Rosa grimaced.

"After what Virginia did," Andi said, "I don't want to forgive her or even look at her. And I've lost any chance of ever getting Mr. Foster to like me." She slumped. "Did you notice I got another failing mark in geography this morning?"

Rosa started on another tamale. "I noticed."

Andi propped her elbows on her knees and rested her chin in her hands. "That's the second time I've gotten low marks this term. Mother's not going to like it. Mr. Foster expects each of us to know all the answers when we recite. I can't remember all those boring facts about rivers, mountains, exports, and imports in South America."

"Virginia knows all the answers," Rosa said.

Andi rolled her eyes. "Virginia's at the top of every class, from arithmetic to spelling. She's so smart, she makes the rest of us look like dunces. I don't know if she's a good student because she enjoys learning, or because she likes to show off, or if she's afraid of failing because her father's the schoolmaster." She paused in thought. "A couple of years ago, when Miss Hall was out sick, the school board took over our class for two weeks. When it was Justin's turn, the kids teased me about being teacher's pet. I felt I had to do everything right or Justin would be shamed." She shuddered. "It was a lousy two weeks."

"And you think Virginia feels the same about her father?"

"I don't know. Maybe. I've heard some of the kids call her worse than teacher's pet. I just know that she's a different person when Mr.

Foster's not around." She sighed. "I'd feel sorry for her and try harder to be a friend if she hadn't gotten me into so much trouble with Chad because of her stupid lies."

"She does not want to be your friend, Andi," Rosa said bluntly.

Andi accepted another tamale. "I know, but my mother thinks Virginia is lonely and unhappy. She wants me to try to be friends with her—you know, the Golden Rule and all that."

Rosa wrinkled her brow. "*¿Cómo?*"

In quick, forbidden Spanish, Andi explained the meaning of the English words. Rosa nodded her approval. "The *señora* is wise."

"Actually, my mother didn't think of it. She got it from the Bible." Andi grinned and bit into her tamale.

"Hey, Andi!" A breathless Cory Blake raced up, interrupting the girls' conversation. "Come play ball. The teams are uneven. We need you." He reached out and grabbed Andi by the arm. The tamale went flying.

Andi shook herself loose from his grasp. "I don't want to play." She hadn't played ball since she'd broken the window the week before.

"You've been moping around all morning," Cory complained. "All on account of that dumb old Virginia Foster. A good, fast ball game is just what you need."

Rosa laughed. "He is right, *amiga*. You are happy when you run and play ball."

"Oh, all right." Andi jumped up and brushed off the back of her skirt. Then she flicked a quick glance toward the half-open doorway at the top of the steps, just to make sure Mr. Foster wasn't spying on her. He wasn't.

But Virginia apparently was. She stood, half-hidden in the shadows behind the door, her dark gaze riveted on Andi and her friends. Her face peeked out through the opening, and her fingers gripped the edge of the door. Two spots of pink colored her pale cheeks.

"I heard you, Andrea Carter," she burst out, throwing open the door. "I heard you and your friends talking about me. You're mean and thoughtless. But it's nothing I didn't expect from this horde of uncultured, backward Westerners." She looked ready to cry.

Andi felt her own cheeks burn. She couldn't remember all she'd said to Rosa, but Cory's "dumb old Virginia Foster" echoed fresh in her mind. What would Mother say if she knew about her unkindness? And after explaining the Golden Rule to Rosa, too! Andi opened her mouth to apologize, but what came out was, "Why did you lie about the accident being my fault on Saturday?"

"I—I didn't," Virginia protested feebly. "You should have warned me about that horse."

"You should have told me you can't ride."

"I *can* ride," Virginia said. "But not a wild, half-broke horse."

Andi laughed out loud at Virginia's outrageous claim. Half-broke horse? Ridiculous! It wasn't Pal's fault his rider was a ninny. "Anybody with a lick of sense and the teeniest bit of horsemanship can ride Pal. You couldn't, and he knew it." She suddenly didn't feel like apologizing. Instead, she turned and clattered down the remaining steps. "Come on, Cory. Let's go."

It was a terrific game. Andi's drooping spirits soared, just as her friends had promised. It wasn't long until she was so caught up in the ball game that she forgot everything else.

The noon hour flew by. With only five minutes remaining, Cory's team lagged one point behind. He handed Andi the bat and let out a long, serious breath. "This is it. You're up. Davy's on base. There are two outs. Hit him in and we tie. Hit a home run and we win. Hit a window and we're dead. Can you do it?"

Andi brushed a sweaty lock of dark hair from her eyes, looked at the pitcher, and grinned. "Sure." She gripped the bat and swung it up to her shoulder.

Cory returned her grin. "Good luck."

Andi knew it was a good pitch the instant the ball left Johnny's hand. She smacked the ball, tossed the bat aside, and took off running for first base. She crossed first and second amid shouts of encouragement. She was past third base and on her way home when she heard Cory's frantic shout. "Slide, Andi!"

She slid for home plate, sending up a rolling cloud of dust. Her feet touched the plate just seconds before the catcher snagged the ball.

"Safe! We won!" Cory shouted. He helped Andi from the ground and pounded her triumphantly on the back. Dust flew everywhere.

Davy Cooper grabbed her hand and shook it. "Good hit."

"Just lucky," Johnny Wilson muttered.

Andi scowled at Johnny, nodded her thanks to the others, and began slapping the dirt from her skirt. It made her sneeze.

A loud clang from the school bell signaled the end of the noon hour.

"Uh-oh," Cory said, glancing toward the schoolhouse. "You don't want to be marked tardy. Better hurry."

"I'm going as fast as I can." She quickly brushed the fine powder from her sleeves and sneezed again.

Cory bit his lip. "You're . . . um . . . awfully dirty, Andi. I wonder what the teacher'll say."

"I know what my father will say," Virginia piped up from the cluster of students watching the game. Everyone turned to stare at her in surprise. "He'll say he's never seen such a dreadful sight. Then he'll probably send her home from school."

Andi's stomach clenched. Virginia's words stung—mostly because they were true. The schoolmaster was going to take a dim view of her unladylike behavior, and it was her own fault. "You needn't rub it in," she said, shaking the dust from her braids.

Virginia stepped forward, wrinkling her nose. "You look like one of those dirty little beggar boys I used to see in the city, roaming the streets and picking through garbage. A shame, really. You come from such a fine family."

Andi straightened up and glared at Virginia. She knew she should turn and walk away. The second bell would be sounding any minute, and she didn't want to be marked tardy. But she didn't move. Neither did any of the other pupils.

"You gonna let her insult you like that, Andi?" Johnny called out with a grin.

Andi wanted nothing more than to rub the snippy girl's nose in the dirt, but she didn't. A young lady did not rub another young lady's nose in the dirt—no matter what. Not even if she lied or said unkind things. A young lady always exhibited self-control, especially if her family name was Carter.

So she drew a deep breath, calmed her pounding heart, and pretended that Virginia's words meant nothing to her. "I guess I'd rather be a dirty beggar," she said with a shrug, "than a liar."

Virginia's eyes grew wide, and her face flamed. Then . . . *smack!* She reached out and slapped Andi across the face.

Andi's hand flew to her stinging cheek. For an instant she could only gape at Virginia. Then the hot, sick feeling in her stomach boiled over and engulfed her. She forgot her promise to her mother. She forgot she was a young lady. She forgot she was a member of a respected family. With a cry of outrage, she flew at Virginia and knocked her to the ground with a resounding *thud.*

Virginia shrieked. A gasp went up from the watching students. Cory groaned.

Andi slammed Virginia onto her back and sat on her just like her brothers would straddle a stubborn calf. "Don't ever hit me again!" she shouted. "Don't lie to me. And stop getting me into trouble with your father. Understand?"

Virginia thrashed weakly and tossed her head from side to side. "You're crushing me," she whimpered. "I—I can't breathe. I'm going to be sick." One flailing hand caught Andi's dress bodice and ripped away part of the lace trim. It dangled in Virginia's face.

"Stop it, Andi!" Cory hollered. He grabbed her arm and dragged her away from Virginia. "The teacher's coming."

Indeed, Mr. Foster was striding purposefully across the schoolyard, glowering. "Why has no one returned to class?" he called out. "The bell rang. Is someone injured?" He pushed his way through the crowd of gawking students. "You will be marked tardy if—" He stopped short at the sight of Andi and Virginia sprawled on the ground. Both girls were covered in fine yellow dust. Virginia was sobbing.

For a moment, Mr. Foster was speechless. Then with a low moan, he flung himself beside his daughter. "Virginia, what happened?"

Virginia clutched at her father and wailed.

Mr. Foster turned accusing eyes on Andi. "What is the meaning of this outrage? Two young ladies—my *daughter*—sitting in the dirt. For shame! Rise at once and return to the schoolroom." Then he rounded on the other students and roared, "All of you. Back to class."

Andi scrambled to her feet, breathing hard. Virginia rose shakily, took a few halting steps, and staggered against her father with a moan. "She called me a liar," she managed between sobs. "She attacked me and sat on me and was beating—"

"You *are* a liar," Andi cut in.

"Enough!" Mr. Foster held Virginia close. "Not another word. I have eyes, and I know very well who's to blame for this incident."

Andi turned and dashed away. Her chest and throat were tight from holding back tears. Her eyes stung. She pushed past her classmates, pounded up the porch steps, and took the narrow stairs two at a time. Then she flung herself into her seat and buried her head in her arms.

The rest of the students tumbled into their places. "Oh, Andi," Maggie whispered from a few rows away, "Mr. Foster's awful mad."

"Yeah, you're really gonna get it." Johnny almost sounded sorry.

"Glad I'm not you," Jack piped up from the seat behind her.

"Shut up, Jack," Cory muttered.

Andi ignored them all.

When Mr. Foster arrived, supporting a hobbling Virginia, Andi raised her head and watched him settle the girl in her desk. She was no longer crying, but her face was streaked with muddy tears and her pale hair tumbled around her face in wild tangles. She did, indeed, look pitiful.

Mr. Foster strode quickly to the front of the room and slammed his palm down onto the top of his desk. "I have never, in all my years of teaching, been witness to such a sight as I saw today. It is a disgrace that a young lady under my instruction should behave in such an unseemly manner." He paused for breath. "Andrea Carter, you make a mockery of your family's good name and their position in this town. You are unruly, short-tempered, and lack any shred of self-control. You have bullied another student, without thought for her delicate constitution. I have no choice but to punish you."

Andi swallowed. She felt sick at the teacher's words—sick, ashamed, and angry. But mostly she was angry. Why was she being singled out when Virginia was guilty as well? Her temper flared, and the warm rush of blood to her cheeks loosened her tongue. "It's true I knocked her down, Mr. Foster. But Virginia slapped me first."

"That's right!" Cory quickly added his support. "Virginia was doing her own share of name calling, and Andi never touched her. It's both their faults."

"Why don't you be fair and punish 'em both?" Jack hollered.

Andi's spirits rose—a little.

Mr. Foster snatched up his ruler and brought it down across his desk with a mighty *whack* where it broke in two. He shook the broken half at Cory and Jack. "Enough." Then he tossed the ruler aside and looked at Andi. "A well-bred young lady does not attack a schoolmate— especially another young lady—no matter what the provocation." He stepped to the corner and took up a long, narrow switch. "Since you have behaved like a rowdy boy, you will be punished as one."

Andi's anger melted into fear. Not the switch! No girl had yet felt the schoolmaster's switch; she definitely didn't want to be the first. Why oh why had she let her temper take over? Why couldn't she have just walked away and let Virginia say what she liked?

Mr. Foster held up the switch. "Rise and pass to the front, Miss Carter."

Andi's throat went dry. She couldn't go up there—she just *couldn't*. No mean-spirited teacher was going to hit her with his nasty old stick. Especially in front of the entire class. "P-please, Mr. Foster," she stammered, "couldn't you send a note home instead?"

"Certainly not. I handle my own disci—" He broke off, his gaze suddenly drawn to the back of the room.

"Leave her alone." The command, crackling with annoyance, turned every head. Chad stood near the stairwell, tall and unsmiling, his arms folded across his chest. His set jaw and icy blue glare told Andi he was more than annoyed—he was furious. She stared at her brother, numb with shock. What was he doing here?

Mr. Foster frowned at Chad. "Mr. Carter, I'm afraid this is none of your affair. The school board put me in charge of this classroom, and I intend to discipline this student as she deserves."

"With that?" Chad made his way to the front of the class and pointed at the switch in Mr. Foster's hand. "I don't care what she's done. Nobody touches my sister with a stick. *Nobody*."

"The school board—of which your brother is a part—gives me the right to do just that. Are you challenging their decision?"

Chad plucked the switch from Mr. Foster's hand. "I guess I am." He snapped it in two and tossed the broken pieces onto the schoolmaster's desk. Then he marched up the aisle. When he got to Andi's desk, he gave her a grim smile. "Come on, little sister. We're leaving."

"Your meddling in my classroom will not go unaddressed at the next school-board meeting," Mr. Foster promised. "And . . ." He nodded at Andi. "Your sister is expelled."

Andi gasped. Expelled! That was a disgrace reserved for the most unruly of pupils. Murmurs of shock and sympathy rippled through the room.

Chad shrugged. "Suit yourself." He took Andi by the arm and steered her toward the stairs. "C'mon, let's get out of here."

Chapter Ten

CONSEQUENCES

Y ou should see yourself," Chad remarked as soon as they were alone. He stood on the schoolhouse porch and lifted the torn bit of trim dangling from Andi's dress. "You're not a pretty sight." He shook his head, released the lace, and clattered down the steps. "Want to tell me what happened?"

Andi hurried after her brother and gave him a quick account of the noon hour. ". . . and then you showed up," she finished breathlessly, coming up beside him. "What were you doing at school, anyway? Not that I'm not grateful, mind you. It was just such a surprise to see you."

Chad grinned and kept walking down the wooden sidewalk. "A nice surprise, I bet."

It was true. Andi had felt utterly alone when she stood before her angry schoolmaster. Chad's unexpected appearance had made her feel warm and safe. She knew he was still angry about his stallion, yet he'd come to her rescue—no questions asked. *Yes*, she decided suddenly, *sometimes it's mighty nice having a big brother—even a bossy one.* She grabbed his hand and gave it a squeeze. "Thanks, Chad."

Chad reached out and ruffled her hair. "I couldn't stand there and let him wallop you, now could I? Not my sweet, pretty, innocent little sister." Now he was teasing her. Andi wasn't innocent, and they both knew it.

She gave him a shove as they crossed a street near the edge of town. "So, why did you come by today? Really? And don't say it was just to rescue me."

"I wanted to tell you and Rosa to stop by the lumberyard after school to catch a ride home with Mitch and me. I guess I'll have to send someone back for Rosa this afternoon." He sighed. "You sure know how to complicate my life."

Andi stopped in her tracks. "Why can't Justin take us home? He didn't go to Sacramento again, did he?"

Chad shook his head. "Not this time. He went to Merced."

Andi looked at him blankly.

"For the murder trial. Remember? Justin's defending that drifter who killed the baggage clerk over at the depot last month." He paused. "Just before school started."

"Oh. *That* trial." Andi shivered—a delicious, scary shiver. The killing of old Mr. Slater had thrown the town of Fresno into a hanging frenzy. Even the children were caught up in it. Jed Hatton was the likely suspect, and Andi had been as disappointed as the rest of the town when the trial was moved safely away to the north. "It sure would be interesting to sit in court and watch Justin prove that Jed didn't kill Mr. Slater, wouldn't it?"

"I suppose," Chad replied carelessly. He started walking.

Andi scurried to catch up. "What's the matter? Don't you think he'll win?"

"Oh, Justin's pretty good in the courtroom, no doubt about it. He might be able to save Jed's scrawny neck." He shrugged. "I just can't figure out why he's defending him in the first place."

"Well . . ." Andi slowed her pace. "Justin says Jed's innocent, but folks have listened to gossip and stirred themselves up to think otherwise." She glanced up at her brother. "Justin's right, isn't he?"

Chad shook his head. "Sorry, Andi, but I don't agree with Justin on this one. I think Jed's guilty." He grasped Andi's sleeve and gave it a tug. "Either way, it's not your concern. You've got your own set of worries—like facing Mother this afternoon." He chuckled.

Andi groaned.

They approached the lumberyard, where Mitch was neatly stacking an assortment of planks and two-by-fours onto the buckboard. Chad waved his approval at the amount of work his brother had accomplished in his absence.

"You sure took your time getting back," Mitch complained, wiping the sweat from his forehead.

"Something more important came up."

"Like what?" He glanced at Andi, who was leaning against the buckboard in gloomy silence. "What are you doing here, sis?"

"I had to rescue our little sister from being thrashed by the new teacher," Chad explained cheerfully. Now that it was over, he certainly seemed to be enjoying the retelling.

Andi wasn't.

Mitch stared at her. "Your teacher was going to thrash you? Why?"

Andi didn't answer. Instead, she climbed on the wheel and slumped against the stack of lumber.

"I rescued her in the nick of time," Chad said. He lifted a bucket of nails into the back. "Go ahead and tell him what you told me, Andi. It's a pretty good story. And no more than that lying Foster girl deserves, if you ask me."

"Nobody's asking you," Andi grumbled. But at Chad's urging, she told Mitch what had happened. By the time she was finished, he was laughing heartily. He wiped the tears from his eyes and leaned against the buckboard for support.

"You sat on her?"

"It's not funny," Andi insisted.

"Not if you don't think so, sis," Mitch agreed quickly, suppressing a smile. He picked up a length of rope and tossed it to Chad, who waited on the other side of the rig.

From her spot on top of the lumber, Andi watched her brothers tie down their load. They didn't appear upset about what would happen when she arrived home. Andi, however, was growing more anxious by the minute. No matter how carefully she gave an account of the incident, her mother wasn't likely to understand. But if one of her brothers was willing to explain, maybe . . .

"Hey, Chad!" She jumped up in her excitement, nearly losing her balance. She caught the back of the seat to steady herself. "Maybe you or Mitch could explain to Mother about my being expelled. I could study my lessons at home. I'd do loads of chores for punishment. You know, like checking fences, flushing out strays, brushing the horses, washing the surrey—"

Chad shook his head. "Sorry, Andi, but you're talking to the wrong brothers. You need a smooth-tongued lawyer to help you out of this fix, and Justin's gone for the week." He secured the rope with one final tug and climbed onto the seat. Grabbing the reins, he released the brake. "Come on, Mitch. Let's forget the rest of our business in town and go home. I'm sure our sister is eager to break the news to Mother."

Andi wasn't eager for any such thing. However, because she didn't want her mother learning about this newest trouble from her teacher, she determined to tell her the first chance she got. She settled herself between her brothers on the hard wooden seat of the buckboard and concentrated on how she could break this dismal news without making it sound as bad as it was.

Within minutes of arriving home, she was sitting on her bed, pouring out the details of her quarrel with Virginia and its disastrous conclusion. When she finished, she held her breath and watched her mother's face for a reaction.

"I thought we agreed you were going to get along with Virginia," Elizabeth commented with a tired sigh.

"I tried," Andi said, near tears. Her mother seemed so disappointed in her. "I really tried. But she lied, and I just . . . well, I lost my temper." She let out a long, slow breath. "I'm sorry, Mother."

"I'm sure you are."

"There's one more thing," Andi whispered, head bowed. "I've been expelled."

Elizabeth stared at her daughter. "Oh, Andrea."

The tears Andi had valiantly held back all day began to trickle down her cheeks. "What am I going to do?"

Elizabeth gathered her daughter in her arms and held her close. She waited quietly until Andi stopped crying. Then she gently stroked her hair. "There's only one thing to do, sweetheart. You have to apologize to Mr. Foster for your behavior."

Andi was silent for a moment. Then she nodded. "I guess I could do that."

"You also need to apologize to Virginia," her mother added softly.

"Mother!" Andi sat up straight. "Virginia slapped me first."

"But you chose the easy way—fighting her back—instead of letting it go. Sometimes it takes more courage *not* to fight." She lifted Andi's chin and smiled at her. "Apologizing is the right thing to do. That will take courage, too." Before Andi could reply, her mother rose from the bed. "I'll take you to school in the morning and try to straighten this all out. I'm sure your teacher is a reasonable man—once he's had time to let things settle."

"I hope so," Andi said fervently.

"However," her mother finished, "if Mr. Foster allows you to return to school, you will wear your very best clothes for the remainder of the week."

Andi groaned. "My very best? I can't do that. I won't be able to play ball or jump rope or anything. I'll have to sit still all week and worry about spoiling a fancy party dress."

Her mother nodded. "I know it will be difficult, but I believe that having to care for your clothes will make you stop and think the next time you find yourself in a similar situation."

Andi sighed, defeated. A young lady all week! How would she ever manage it?

"Mr. Foster?" Elizabeth Carter's voice rang clear and strong in the early morning silence of the classroom.

The schoolmaster glanced up from where he sat correcting papers. "Good morning, Mrs. Carter," he replied pleasantly. With a few quick strides, Mr. Foster made his way up the aisle.

He grasped Elizabeth's hand. "I had a feeling I'd be hearing from you, although I confess I didn't think it would be this soon." He looked at Andi. "I usually do not allow expelled students back into the classroom until I've met with the school board to discuss the situation."

"Justin has gone to Merced for a trial," Elizabeth said, "so it will be at least a week before the board can meet. In the meantime, I prefer that Andrea not miss school. When the board meets, and if they support your decision, then I will be happy to make other arrangements. But for now . . ."—she inclined her head in Andi's direction—"Andrea has something she'd like to say."

"Indeed? It must be something important, seeing that she dressed up for the occasion."

Andi flushed miserably and stared at the floor. No amount of pleading had changed her mother's mind about the clothes she had to wear to school today. Tearfully, she'd put on her best blue satin frock—complete with the required number of hot, scratchy petticoats. She'd brushed and combed her hair to her mother's exacting standards. Now, she stood uneasily before the teacher, armed with a carefully worded apology. She locked her fingers behind her back and prayed for the awkward moment to pass.

"Andrea," her mother prompted.

Andi raised her head and met the teacher's dark eyes. "I'm sorry I lost my temper and knocked Virginia down yesterday. It was wrong of me. I promise it won't happen again. May I come back to school?"

Mr. Foster didn't say anything. Instead, he turned to Elizabeth. "Mrs. Carter, I do not appreciate your son meddling in my classroom."

"I understand," Elizabeth agreed with a solemn nod of her head. "Chad believed he was protecting his sister, but he could have been more diplomatic about it."

Andi looked at her mother in bewilderment. *Diplomatic!* With a stick hanging over his sister's head? "Mother . . . ?"

Elizabeth silenced her with a look. Then she turned back to the schoolmaster. "Do you wish to discipline her now?"

Andi's mouth dropped open. "Mother!" Her mother couldn't possibly be serious!

Mr. Foster appeared as astonished as Andi at the offer. "Thank you, Mrs. Carter. I appreciate your cooperation." He folded his arms across his chest and smiled—something Andi had seen him do only once or twice since school started. "However, I don't believe that will be necessary. It appears that your punishment more than fits the crime." Turning to Andi, he said, "Yes, Miss Carter, I accept your apology. You may return to school—for now."

"Thank you," Andi muttered. Mr. Foster was obviously enjoying her discomfort.

Elizabeth returned the schoolmaster's smile. "I can assure you that Andrea's behavior in class this week will be exemplary. Good day, Mr. Foster."

"Good day, Mrs. Carter, and thank you."

Elizabeth left, leaving Andi alone to face the embarrassment of her classmates' stares as they all filed into the schoolroom. *This is definitely not going to be a good week*, she decided, scratching at a particularly hot and itchy spot on her leg. She bit her lip and prepared to endure the next four days, when she would finally be free from her prison of ruffles and lace.

Chapter Eleven

NEWS

With a relief bordering on tears, Andi pulled on her regular school clothes the following Monday. She glanced toward her open wardrobe and gave her Sunday frocks a mock salute. "*Adios*, and good riddance." She crossed over to the small vanity and quickly brushed out her hair, tying it back sloppily with a length of blue ribbon.

"Andi Carter," she announced to her cheerful reflection, "you have just been paroled." She gave an approving glance around her room. For once, it was neat and clean. No dirty clothes or forgotten horse tack lay in a corner. The top of her bureau was tidy and the drawers closed. She drew back the curtains and opened the doors onto the balcony. A pleasant fall breeze blew across her face.

Andi left her room and skipped down the hall. She paused at the top of the stairs; the banister beckoned to her. She ran her hand along the polished wooden railing and sighed. *One time*, she reasoned.

"Don't you dare!" Melinda called from her bedroom doorway. She hurried over. "You know how it upsets Luisa. She's certain you're going to break an arm or a leg with all that sliding."

Andi peered down the wide staircase. The Carters' fiery little housekeeper was nowhere in sight. Before Melinda could stop her, she settled herself onto the railing and sailed down in happy abandon. Her delight turned to unexpected pain a moment later when she landed on the foyer floor with a resounding *thud*.

"Ouch!" She scrambled hastily to her feet and rubbed her sore backside.

"Serves you right," Melinda scolded from the top of the stairs. She grinned. "But it did look like fun."

Both girls were giggling when they entered the dining room.

"Good morning." Andi beamed.

"Are you responsible for the loud noise we just heard?" her mother asked, calmly sipping her coffee.

Andi pulled out a chair and sat down. "Yes, Mother. I couldn't help it. I woke up so happy, I had to slide—just this once."

"So, your prison sentence is over," said Chad.

"You bet it is. Never have I spent a longer week in school. But Mr. Foster smiled at me twice and remarked on my improved character." She scooted her chair closer to the table and reached for her milk. "I think he was surprised to learn I'd actually apologized to Virginia."

"So, you and Virginia are on good terms?" Melinda asked.

"Not exactly. I apologized like I was supposed to, but she wouldn't forgive me." Andi shrugged. "I don't care. I'm just going to make sure I do the right thing from now on." She took a long drink of milk and glanced around the table for something to eat. "Hi, Justin. You're finally home. Could you please pass the eggs?"

Justin didn't seem to hear the request. He was staring intently at the cup of coffee in his hand.

"Justin," Andi repeated, a little louder. He looked up. "The eggs, please." She pointed to them.

"Oh, I'm sorry. Here you go." He passed her a heaping platter of scrambled eggs. "I heard you had an interesting week at school," he commented before going back to contemplating his coffee cup.

"It was a terrible week." Andi slid a generous portion of eggs onto her plate and continued to chatter. "Maggie and Rachel acted like they'd never seen me in a fancy dress before. They wore me out with all their silly admiration. I would've gladly swapped clothes with them if I could've gotten away with it." She spared a quick glance at her mother, who only smiled and continued with her breakfast.

"Cory had a conniption fit when he saw I wasn't going to be any good for his ball game. He really got sore when his team lost every game. And that horrid Johnny Wilson teased me and pulled my hair a dozen times. He is such a bully. I wish he—" She broke off. Justin obviously wasn't listening.

"Hmm," he finally remarked. He shook his head and stared out through the French doors leading to the patio.

Andi followed his gaze. "Something wrong, Justin?"

"Is it the trial?" their mother asked softly.

Justin put down his coffee cup and nodded. "The verdict has been eating away at me since I left Merced. I didn't sleep much last night."

"Jed Hatton was convicted?"

"Yes." He closed his eyes and sighed.

Andi ate her breakfast in silence, listening to every word. She was sorry her brother had lost his case. He looked tired and sad.

"Come on, Justin," Chad said impatiently. "You did your job the best you could. The jury made the decision. It's not your fault." He helped himself to more eggs. "Besides," he added with a satisfied smile, "I always figured he was guilty."

"Oh, you did, did you?" Justin's voice turned bitter. "Well, I still believe he's innocent. His trial was about as fair as a lynch mob. Public opinion had him hung before the trial ever began." He lowered his fist to the table with a bang. "I tore the witness's story apart. I should have been able to convince the jury, yet they found him guilty."

"Don't kick yourself," Mitch broke in. "What more could you have done? He got the best lawyer in California, didn't he?"

"Will he hang?" Andi burst out. Wouldn't that be something to tell the kids at school!

"Andrea, that will do," her mother warned with a frown.

Justin turned to his sister. "No, he won't hang. The judge sentenced him to life in prison."

"There you go, Justin," Chad insisted. "With any other lawyer he'd probably have gotten a noose. You saved his worthless hide. Jed should be—"

A loud knock at the front door interrupted the brothers. Everyone turned when the sheriff walked into the dining room.

"Russ!" Chad called out in greeting. "Pull up a chair. You're just in time for breakfast."

Sheriff Tate shook his head. "Not this morning." He turned to Justin. "I hate to tell you this, but Jed Hatton escaped last night on his way to prison."

"Last night?" Justin exclaimed. "Where is he now?"

"I don't know. Rumor has it he's armed and headed this way."

"Armed?" Justin shook his head. "That's not good."

"No, it's not," the sheriff agreed with a frown.

"But why?" Melinda asked.

Sheriff Tate shrugged. "Who knows? Maybe he wants to make trouble for the witness who spoke against him."

Justin looked stunned. "I told him I was going to appeal. Why couldn't he be patient?"

"He won't stand a chance of an appeal if he comes back to Fresno hunting trouble," the sheriff said. He turned to Mitch and Chad. "You boys got time this morning to help search the town—just in case the rumors are true?"

"A couple of things around here can't wait," Chad replied. "But we'll join you as soon as we can."

"Fine," Russ agreed. He replaced his hat and nodded as he left. "Better be on my way. Good morning, ladies. See you boys later."

Chad threw down his napkin and stood up. "Well, little brother," he said to Mitch, "looks like a busy day. Let's take care of things so we can get to town." He nodded to the family. "See you this evening, Mother, girls."

"'Bye," Mitch said. They left in a hurry.

Justin drained the rest of his coffee in one gulp. "I guess I'd better head to town early this morning. I don't intend to let this town string Jed up."

"You know Sheriff Tate won't stand for a lynching," Elizabeth calmly reminded her son.

"I hope you're right." He turned to Andi. "You ready to go?"

Andi sat up abruptly at the question and glanced down at her partially eaten breakfast. She'd been so intent on listening, she'd forgotten all about eating. Quickly, she scooped up a forkful of eggs. "Can you wait a couple of minutes?"

"Not this morning. You heard the sheriff. I'm leaving right now. Perhaps you and Rosa can ride Taffy and Pal into town."

"What a great idea!" Andi exclaimed. "Could we, Mother?"

"I don't know, Andrea. It's a long way for you girls."

"Please? Justin thinks it's a good idea."

Justin nodded. "I'll make arrangements with Sam Blake to board the horses for the day."

"All right," Elizabeth gave in. "But no shortcuts through anyone's orchards or fields. You stay on the road."

"Yes, ma'am," Andi agreed. Not that her mother's reluctance made any sense. She could ride all over the ranch for miles on end without anyone saying a word, but it practically took a miracle to be allowed to ride into town on her own. "I think you should leave early for work more often," she suggested to Justin.

"Now, I like that," he teased. "You'd trade my company for that of a horse?"

Andi giggled at her brother's comment. "Don't try to make me feel guilty. I never have time to ride Taffy these days."

"You're right, honey," Justin agreed with a wink. "Have a wonderful time."

Chapter Twelve

THE UNWELCOME VISITOR

Andi's joy bubbled over at the idea of riding into town on Taffy. She expressed her delight by challenging Rosa to a horse race. Rosa gritted her teeth and nodded. Andi knew her friend's willingness to race was a sign of true loyalty. To show her gratefulness, she gave Rosa a five-minute head start.

The road along the valley floor was straight and flat—perfect for racing. As Andi galloped toward town in typical breakneck fashion, she shouted and laughed and sang at the top of her voice. The memory of her past miserable week melted away, replaced with the pleasure of just knowing she was alive on such a beautiful fall morning.

She caught up with Rosa a few miles from town. The girls cooled down their mounts and visited together until they reached Blake's livery stable, where the horses would be boarded for the day.

Cory called to the girls as they were leaving the livery. "Wait a minute, and I'll walk with you." He snatched up his books and lunch-pail and ran to catch up. "I see you rode—or rather, raced—Taffy to town," he commented, nodding toward the sweaty horses. "Pa'll charge you extra for the rubdown, you know."

Andi stepped out into the sunshine. "It's worth it. I had a fine ride."

"Lucky," Cory said. "How'd you talk your ma into letting you ride to town?"

Andi quickly told him about the sheriff's visit to the ranch.

"Jed Hatton!" Cory crowed. "Guilty? And escaped? This is the

91

most exciting news around here since Frank Williams found that forty-ounce gold nugget up at Coarse Gold Gulch last spring."

Andi agreed.

Cory sighed. "I reckon they'll catch ol' Jed today while we're in school. We'll miss all the excitement—like always. Maybe I'll play hooky and join the search."

Andi reached for Cory just as the first bell rang. "Better not," she warned, tugging on his shirtsleeve. Then she grinned. "I'll race you to school."

All three took off at a run. They were laughing and gasping for breath when they hit the porch of the schoolhouse and started up the stairs to the classroom.

By the time the second bell rang out its warning to tardy students, Andi was seated quietly beside Rosa. She folded her hands, placed them on her desk, and gave the teacher a cheerful smile when he passed her seat. *This week*, she determined silently, *Mr. Foster will find no fault with my behavior.*

"Class will come to order," Mr. Foster announced, stepping to the front of the schoolroom. Everyone rose. He opened the day with his customary reading of a psalm. "I will lift up mine eyes unto the hills, from whence cometh my help. . . ." As usual, his droning voice ruined what should have been an inspiring portion of Scripture.

When everyone was seated, Mr. Foster announced the morning's first assignment. "Take out your copybooks and copy the passage from the board. As always, I expect your best effort, your neatest penmanship."

Andi pulled her copybook from her desk and frowned. Penmanship assignments were a sore trial to her. They were so boring. She had less than a dozen perfect pages in her entire tablet—a fact Mr. Foster did not find amusing. Usually, she let her fingers form the tedious letters while her thoughts traveled far away, resulting in a great many unsightly inkblots. *Today I'll pay attention*, she promised herself. Taking a deep breath, she dipped her pen into the inkwell and started copying the selection from the board as neatly and carefully as she could.

Absorbed in proving she could finish an entire page without making one mistake, Andi didn't hear the commotion at the back of the room ten minutes later. She didn't notice the sudden rustling of skirts and the nervous whispering of her classmates. It wasn't until Cory jabbed her in the back and whispered, "Andi," that she returned her attention to her surroundings. Then she groaned. Near the bottom of the page a dark, wet blob of ink now marred the perfectly formed letters of her last sentence.

"Cory!" she snapped, whirling on the boy. She didn't care if Mr. Foster punished her for her outburst. "You made me ruin my—"

Cory clapped a hand over Andi's mouth and gestured behind his shoulder, toward the back of the room.

Andi glanced past her friend's blond head and stared. Slowly, Cory removed his hand from Andi's mouth and returned his own gaze to the back of the classroom. Every student sat transfixed, watching the strange man standing nervously near the staircase.

He was tall and heavyset, with dark eyes. Lank, muddy-brown hair fell over his ears. He scratched at his unshaven chin and glanced around the room. A frown creased his forehead. With a trembling hand, he pulled a large pistol from the waistband of his pants. "You all sit real still, and nobody'll get hurt," he said.

Andi gulped back her surprise and dug her fingers into her friend's arm. "Cory," she whispered, "you know who that is? It's—it's Jed Hat—"

Cory's hand flew to cover Andi's mouth once more. "Shhh! Don't say nothin' to aggravate him. He's a dangerous killer."

She peeled Cory's fingers from her face and leaned over his desk. "He doesn't look dangerous. He looks scared. You'd be, too, if you were headed to prison for something you didn't do."

"He murdered Mr. Slater," Cory insisted in a low voice.

"No, he didn't. Justin says he—"

"Enough chatter!" Jed's voice cracked like a rifle shot. "All of you. Quit yer gawkin' and turn around."

Andi spun around and faced the front of the classroom. She wondered what Mr. Foster was thinking. He sat behind his desk, unmoving, his expression carved from stone. Andi couldn't tell if her teacher's face was white with anger or pale with fright.

Jed grunted his satisfaction and hurried up the aisle toward the schoolmaster. When he reached the front of the room, Mr. Foster rose from behind his desk and confronted Jed as if he were an erring student. "What is the meaning of this intrusion? How dare you pull a gun on these children! Leave at once."

The stranger looked surprised, but recovered quickly. He stepped around the desk and backhanded the schoolmaster across the face. Several students gasped. Virginia shrieked. Mr. Foster collapsed into his chair, dazed. Blood trickled from a corner of his mouth.

"I told everybody to sit still and keep quiet. That goes for you, too," Jed said. "I got no patience for fools today." Quickly, he whirled on the class. "If any of you are thinkin' of makin' a run for it while I'm not lookin', think again. You'll end up like your teacher here." He pointed a finger at tall, red-haired Seth Atkins sitting in the seat nearest the stairs. "You got any fool notions 'bout leavin', boy?"

"N-no, sir."

"Good." Jed found an unoccupied desk in the front row, lifted his foot to the seat, and rested his gun across his knee. He began to relax. "In case you're wonderin' why I'm here, I'll tell you. The whole town's lookin' for me, and I need a place to hide. They think I killed a fella. Well, I didn't kill nobody, and I ain't gonna let nobody haul me off to prison." He jerked his head in the direction of the four large windows lining the side of the schoolroom. "This place's got a good view of the town. Nobody can sneak up without me knowin' 'bout it." He crossed to one of the windows and glanced outside. Then he returned to the front of the classroom. "And if things go sour . . ." He raised his gun. "I got me a fine bunch of hostages."

Andi cringed at the word *hostages*. The more she listened to Jed and watched the way he acted, the less she believed him innocent of killing poor Mr. Slater. But, she reasoned to herself, fear sometimes does strange things to people. She knew she often used anger to keep others from knowing she was afraid. Perhaps Jed was using meanness to hide his own fear.

The teacher dabbed at his swollen, bloody lip with a large white handkerchief. "You can't hide in here forever," he said. In spite of his obvious pain and fear, Mr. Foster spoke calmly and sensibly. "The children must be allowed to go home at the end of the day."

"Nobody goes 'til I say so," Jed snapped, "and I say we wait. In a few hours, when they're tired of searchin', I can sneak away. Until then, go on about your business and don't give me no trouble."

Andi swallowed her uneasiness and bent over her copybook. The dried inkblot stared up at her. Her anger at Cory for ruining her perfect page of penmanship now seemed silly. She slammed the copybook shut and reached for her speller. But she couldn't concentrate. Her thoughts were too mixed up to care about the lesson she should be studying.

She frowned. *Why would Jed take the chance of coming back to town? He should've run far, far away. He must not be thinking straight. If only Justin were here! He could help Jed. He'd fix everything.*

A muffled sob brought Andi out of her musing. She glanced at Rosa. Her friend was hunched over her reader. Two large tears splattered onto the page. Andi reached over and patted her friend on the back. "Don't cry, Rosa," she whispered. "I know it doesn't look like it, but Justin says Jed's innocent. He won't hurt us, not so long as we're quiet and do what he says."

Rosa nodded and rubbed her eyes. She gave Andi a halfhearted smile.

The morning dragged. Jed circled the room, weaving up and down the aisles like an over-attentive schoolmaster. Each time he passed the windows, he peered cautiously outside. Then, with a sigh and a grunt, he continued making his way around the classroom.

By midmorning his movements had settled into a mind-numbing routine. The sound of his heavy boots clomping up and down the aisles was a constant reminder of his unwelcome presence. Occasionally, he stopped near a desk, hiked his boot up onto the seat of a frightened boy or girl, and rested his gun hand across his knee.

Andi watched Jed. When he stopped at her desk and shoved his booted toe onto her seat, she forced herself to ignore him. *He can't frighten me*, she decided, and calmly turned a page in her geography book. Jed laughed softly, gave a lock of her hair a quick, painful tweak, and moved on.

It was close to noon when Jed completed another dreary circle of the schoolroom. He stifled a yawn and peered out the window, like he had done a dozen times earlier that morning.

All of a sudden, he uttered a curse and leaped away from the window. "A couple o' men are headed this way! Looks like that sheriff ain't gonna give up 'til he searches every building, shed, and privy in this town." His dark, worried eyes searched the classroom. "This ain't workin' like I planned," he mumbled, pacing the room.

Mr. Foster stood up. "Let me talk to the sheriff's men. I'll tell them there's no need to search the school. You were here, but you left an hour ago. When the men leave, you'll have a chance to make your escape."

Jed stopped his pacing and looked at Mr. Foster with fresh interest. "You serious, Teach? You'd do that?"

Mr. Foster nodded and started for the stairs. "Yes. For the children's sake, so you'll leave this classroom."

Suddenly, Virginia leaped from her seat and flew after her father. "Don't leave me, Father!" She threw her arms around his waist and clung to him. "I'm frightened. Take me with you."

Before Mr. Foster could react, Jed rushed up the aisle and snatched Virginia by the arm. He pressed a rough hand over her mouth and pulled her close. "This your little gal, Teach?"

Mr. Foster's gaze was riveted on his daughter. He drew a shaky hand across his forehead and nodded. "Please don't hurt her."

"Just deliver the message."

"I'll be right back, Virginia," he assured her. Then he disappeared down the stairs.

An eerie silence settled over the classroom while they waited for the teacher's return. Virginia was trembling violently in Jed's grasp. Her huge eyes, fixed on Andi, pleaded for help.

Do you know what kind of fix you're in now? Andi wanted to shout at the silly girl. *You've given Jed the perfect hostage.*

Andi tore her gaze away from the frightened girl. She had a feeling Virginia knew—too late—the danger she'd put herself in. It made her helplessness heart-wrenching to watch. *Please, God,* Andi pleaded silently, *hurry up and bring Mr. Foster back to class, before Virginia dies of fright.* She squeezed her eyes shut and tried to forget the look in the captive girl's eyes. It was no use. All she saw behind her closed eyelids was Virginia's despair.

Mr. Foster's return to the classroom a few minutes later made Andi want to cry out in relief. Perhaps Jed would leave now.

"Well?" Jed snarled, keeping a tight grip on Virginia. "What happened?"

Mr. Foster kept his attention on his daughter as he returned to his desk. "I think they believed me," he said, sinking into his chair. "They asked which way you went. I told them you headed west—toward the railroad depot." He drew a deep breath. "Please let my daughter go. You should leave right now, while the search party is—"

"Don't tell me my business!" Jed shoved Virginia away. She scurried to her father and threw herself at him, sobbing wildly. Mr. Foster held her close.

Jed moved quickly toward the stairs. Just before he started down, he whirled on the schoolmaster and raised his gun. "You better hope those men believed you, or somebody's gonna be very, very sorry." He turned and vanished down the long, narrow stairway.

Suddenly, a loud, clear voice called Jed's name from outside. Andi's heart leaped with hope. Justin had come! Then, just as quickly, her heart settled to her stomach in a cold, hard lump. *Now Jed's trapped*, she realized. *And so are we.*

Chapter Thirteen

THE PERFECT HOSTAGE

J ed clattered up the stairs and burst back into the classroom, his expression a mixture of fury and terror. He raced up the aisle, snatched Virginia from her father, and pulled her against him in a rib-crushing hold. Virginia gasped. Mr. Foster lunged for her.

Jed shoved him away with a snarl. "You fixed it for me real good!" He edged his way toward the partly open window and peered out, dragging the sobbing Virginia with him. "They didn't believe you for a minute."

"I can't understand it," Mr. Foster protested weakly. He shook his head. "I told them exactly what—"

"Jed Hatton!" Justin shouted from the schoolyard below. His voice carried clearly into the classroom. "It's Justin Carter. I'm unarmed. Let me come up and talk to you. We can work something out."

Listen to him! Andi wanted to shout, but she held her tongue and turned to see what Jed would do. He was trying to watch the classroom, look out the window, and keep control of Virginia, all at the same time. The poor girl whimpered and twisted and begged to be set free, all the while crying for her father.

Mr. Foster stepped forward.

"Stay put." Jed turned and shouted to the men outside, "It's no use, lawyer. I know you tried, and I ain't holdin' it against you, but it's too late. You said the jury wouldn't find me guilty, but they did."

"It's *not* too late," Justin argued. "We can appeal. But it won't work with you up there, holding those kids. You've got to give yourself up. Let me help you, Jed. I promise no one will hurt you."

99

Jed was silent a moment. He scowled at Virginia and dug his fingers into her arm. "Hush! I can't think with all that sniveling." He returned to the open window. "Let me study on it a bit."

"All right," Justin agreed quickly. "Take your time."

No one said a word. Even Virginia, pale and shaking, stopped crying while Jed chewed on his lip and pondered the situation. His gaze traveled around the classroom, flickered briefly at the sight of the open stairway, then rested on Virginia. He clenched his jaw, and his eyes grew hard.

Andi could see Jed's sudden determined look from where she sat, two rows away. With a sinking heart, she realized he had no intention of talking to Justin. *He's going to run!* She caught her breath. *He's going to take Virginia and run.*

Jed finally spoke, confirming Andi's guess. "I ain't listenin' to any lawyer's clever words. Nope. I reckon I got a better chance if I take along this little lady here." He squeezed Virginia's arm. "You're perfect. The teacher's gal. Just what I need to get me out of town in one piece." He gave her a jerk. "Come on, let's go."

Virginia drew a sharp, frantic breath at Jed's words and tried to tear herself from his crushing grip. "No. Not me. Oh, please! Father, don't let him take me." She gulped for air and thrashed wildly at Jed. Her voice rose to a shriek. "Father!"

"Mr. Hatton!" The schoolmaster rose to his feet and pleaded, "My daughter—she's delicate. Her health is not good. If you take her, she'll become ill. She's not used to the roughness of this country. I beg you, sir, don't—"

Jed aimed his pistol at Mr. Foster's chest. "Sit down an' shut up." Mr. Foster sat. Jed gave Virginia a rough, one-handed shake. "Don't you see I got no choice? Now, stop your bawlin' and get hold of yourself." Virginia cried louder. "I mean it, girl. If you don't shut up, I'm gonna slap you."

Virginia's desperate cries for help echoed in Andi's ears until she could hardly breathe. She looked at the teacher. He sat at his desk, clenching and unclenching his fists and staring, wild-eyed, at his daughter. He looked out of his mind with worry.

You're her father! Andi screamed silently. *You know she can't go with Jed. Why don't you do something?*

You do something, a quiet voice whispered in her head.

Me? I can't, Andi protested to herself. *I'm just a girl. What can I do? I can't run up and snatch Jed's gun away. I'm scared, too. Surely God doesn't expect me to—*

The sound of a sharp slap and Virginia's scream yanked Andi from her mental seesaw. She sprang to her feet, propelled by the anguish she heard in Virginia's voice. "Stop it!"

Jed's hand froze in midair. He spun around and gaped at Andi. Then he dropped his hand to his side. The next slap never came. Virginia fainted. She slumped to the floor and lay in a heap at Jed's feet.

Andi glanced around the room. Everyone was staring at her in astonishment. She was just as surprised as her classmates to find herself the center of attention. She didn't know what to do or say, so she said the first thing that came to her mind.

"Please don't take Virginia with you. She'd be no use to you at all. Look at her. She fainted. She does it all the time. And she can't ride. You wouldn't make it a mile from town before she tumbled right off the horse. That'd slow you down, wouldn't it?" Andi paused for breath. She knew she was babbling. Her sentences tumbled out, one on top of the other. *Jed's looking at me like I'm a lunatic. What do I do now?*

The answer struck like lightning.

"Take me, instead," she blurted out. "I promise I won't cry or faint."

Jed Hatton's mouth fell open.

Andi's unexpected offer brought Mr. Foster to life. "Andrea, sit down," he ordered sharply. He hurried over to where Virginia lay and rested a protective hand on her head. "Mr. Hatton, none of these children will leave the classroom. I will not allow it. Your only chance—" The smash of a gun-butt against his head sent the teacher sprawling to the floor next to his daughter, unconscious.

"Interferin' fool," Jed muttered. He returned his attention to Andi. "So, you want to take this ninny's place?"

Andi swallowed and stared at Jed, tongue-tied with fear. *What have I done?* She glanced at the two unconscious people lying crumpled at Jed's feet and sighed. She knew what she'd done. It was simple. Virginia was a tenderfoot, a newcomer to the Valley; she knew nothing about surviving outside of town. She was without a doubt the most unlikable, snippy, and lying girl Andi had ever met, but she was also lonely, insecure, and frightened to death. She didn't deserve to be dragged through the wild by a scruffy, escaped prisoner—even if he *was* innocent.

Andi set her jaw. Perhaps she'd been hasty with her decision, but nobody else was jumping in to lend a hand. It looked like it was up to her. Taking Virginia's place was the right thing to do, no matter how scared she was.

With a deep breath, she squared her shoulders and faced Jed. "Yes. Take me."

"If that ain't the craziest thing I've heard." Jed shook his head. "No thanks. I'm better off with this snivelin' little lady, though she'll no doubt give me trouble. You got gumption, girl, I'll give you that, but I need somebody important, like this teacher's gal." He prodded Virginia with the toe of his boot. She had revived and was staring at Andi with tear-filled, hopeful eyes.

"My brother's your lawyer," Andi challenged, angry at Jed's tone. "Is that important enough for you?"

Jed's eyes opened wide. "I reckon it is." He yanked Virginia to her feet and pushed her down the aisle ahead of him until she stood beside Andi. Grabbing Andi by the arm, he shoved Virginia away. "I don't need you no more."

Virginia stumbled and fell into Andi's seat.

Jed grinned at Andi. "You really Justin Carter's sister?"

Andi nodded.

"Well, that's mighty fine, girl. Mighty fine. You reckon your brother'll give me what I want when he sees I've got you?"

Andi bristled and jerked her arm free. "I guess you'll just have to ask him and find out."

Jed chuckled. "You're full of sass, girl. That's good." He gripped her arm once more. "Let's go."

Andi noted the satisfied gleam in Jed Hatton's dark eyes, took a deep breath, and allowed herself to be pulled to the back of the room and down the stairs. Her stomach lurched in fear. *There's nothing to be afraid of,* she scolded herself. *Jed's innocent. Justin said so. Justin'll take care of everything.* But her stomach continued to churn.

Jed cracked open the door of the schoolhouse. "Hey, Carter!"

"I'm listening," Justin said.

Andi peeked through the opening and gasped. A crowd of eager-looking citizens—armed with everything from old shotguns to shiny Winchester rifles and pearl-handled six-shooters—lined the dusty street across from the grammar school. Justin and Sheriff Tate stood in the schoolyard, no more than a dozen yards away, their attention fixed on the schoolhouse.

Jed whistled at the sight. "I'll make this quick, lawyer. I'm holdin' a girl here who says she's your sister. If you got any feelings for her, you clear out all these trigger-happy folks and find us a couple o' horses and some grub. Then me and the little lady'll ride out real peaceful-like."

"No, Jed!" Justin's voice betrayed his shock and dismay. "That's not the answer. Don't destroy your chance for an appeal by doing something so stupid. Your best bet is to throw out your gun and let me come inside and talk. I know you're not a killer. We have a chance—a *good* chance. Don't throw it away because you're scared."

"Quit yer jabberin'. All I want is a couple o' horses and some supplies. Are you gonna get 'em or not?"

"All right," Justin said. "We'll do it."

Jed opened the door wider and poked his head out. "Glad to hear that. I reckon we'll—"

A bullet cracked into the doorpost. It sent splinters of wood into Jed's face and into Andi's hair. Jed slammed the door shut. Then he reached for Andi and gave her a rough shake. "Is your brother fool enough to want to see you dead?"

"Justin didn't do it!" Andi insisted, stifling a sob.

"Maybe not, but somebody did." With a shaking arm, he crushed Andi to him and kicked open the door. "Lawyer, you nearly got us both shot." He raised his gun and made his way down the porch steps and into the hot, dusty schoolyard. "Now, keep all these gun-totin' fools away and bring me my horses and supplies, or something bad's gonna happen to this girl."

"Take it easy, Jed," Justin said quickly, holding up his hands. "That shot was fired by accident. It won't happen again. We're going for the horses."

Sheriff Tate motioned to a couple of his deputies and whispered his orders. They took off immediately. Then he raised his voice to the onlookers. "There's nothing for you to do here. You folks can go about your business." When nobody moved, the sheriff repeated his orders in a louder tone. "You hear me? Clear out." The crowd reluctantly dispersed.

Andi shaded her eyes against the brightness of the noon sun. Why did Justin look so—so scared? Her oldest brother was strong and smart. He always had the right answers. He always knew what to do. He'd be able to convince Jed to let her go . . . wouldn't he?

"Justin?" she ventured. He motioned her to be quiet.

Jed was speaking. "Listen, Mr. Carter. I'm sorry it had to be your sister. I grabbed me the teacher's gal—a snivelin' little thing—but she was fixin' to be real trouble. This gal here felt sorry for her and offered to take her place. When she told me she was your sister, I couldn't pass it up."

"Let her go, Jed," Justin demanded. "You don't need her. Take me. I'll go with you for as long as you like. We can talk. Just you and me. When you feel safe, we'll come back together and start the appeal. Or," he offered, "you can leave me along the road and be on your way." He spread his hands in sincerity. "I give you my word."

Jed shook his head. "No deal. I've already had me an earful of your fancy words and I don't want no more." He tightened his grip on Andi. "Now, where are the horses?"

Justin's shoulders slumped. "They're on their way."

The next few minutes seemed like an eternity to Andi. Crushed against Jed until she couldn't take a deep breath, she watched her brother and wondered why he didn't do anything to help her. He stood scarcely a stone's throw away, yet he made no effort to speak to Jed or to her. In fact, he looked very much like Mr. Foster had looked a few minutes before—frightened and helpless.

Alarmed at the similarities between them, she burst out, "Justin, why don't you do something?" Then she realized that Mr. Foster had tried to do something, and he was lying unconscious on the schoolroom floor.

"I'm sorry, honey," Justin said softly. "I tried. But the only way I can protect you now is by doing exactly what Jed says. As long as you and I remember that, he won't hurt you. You'll be safe." He nodded at Jed. "Isn't that right, Jed?"

Jed grinned. "You betcha. I wouldn't think of hurtin' a hair on this gal's head, so long as she behaves herself and gives me no trouble. I like her. She showed more gumption than anybody else in that schoolroom. We'll get along just fine, I reckon. I might even let her go, once I'm in the clear." He broke into a broad smile as two horses, led by the sheriff's deputy, were brought to a halt in front of him.

Andi stared at the horses in wonder. She didn't know how the sheriff had arranged it, but Taffy stood next to a pinto gelding—saddled, bridled, and ready to go. She felt her spirits rise at this unexpected gift.

"Well, it looks like we'll be headin' out." Jed led his hostage to Taffy and tossed her onto the mare's back. Then, to Andi's dismay, he pulled himself up behind her and accepted the lead rope of the pinto. He gripped his gun with his free hand and said, "I ain't takin' no chances, little lady. We ride together for a spell."

Andi twisted around and looked at Jed through tear-filled eyes. "May I please say good-bye to my brother?"

"Make it quick."

Andi's throat tightened when she met Justin's grief-stricken gaze. She blinked desperately to hold back her tears. "I'm sorry I made a mess of things, Justin. Tell Mother I love her. Tell her good-bye for me and—and I'll see her soon."

"I will," Justin promised, stepping up to the horse. He ignored Jed's warning look and reached for his sister's hand. "You did the right thing," he assured her. "I'm proud of you. Now, don't be afraid. Be strong. Be brave. And God go with you." He gave her hand a gentle squeeze. "Even if I can't."

Andi nodded and tried to speak. She wanted to tell Justin she'd be strong and brave and anything else he wanted her to be, but the words stuck in her throat. Tears came instead.

Jed raised his pistol. "Step aside, counselor."

Justin dropped Andi's hand and backed away. "I love you," he whispered.

Jed yanked Taffy around and urged her into a gallop. It wouldn't be long before Fresno was far, far behind.

Chapter Fourteen

INTO THE UNKNOWN

Jed galloped Taffy until Andi was sure her horse would collapse from exhaustion. She was furious, but it helped push aside her fear. Many miles south of town, Jed finally slowed the horse to a walk, then stopped. He dismounted but hung onto Taffy's reins.

"Listen here," he said. "I'm mountin' up on this pinto. If you know what's good for you, you'll stay put."

Andi nodded wearily. "Haven't we gone far enough? You've got a good lead by now. You could go a lot faster without me, you know."

"Shut up," Jed ordered. He mounted the pinto and jerked Taffy's reins. The mare leaped forward. Only Andi's ability to react quickly saved her from a nasty spill. She managed to keep her seat, which brought a look of respect from Jed. "Well, little lady, looks like you were the better choice all the way around. We'll make good time, you and me."

"Don't worry about *me*, mister. I can keep up. But I'm not so sure about the horses. You're pushing them too hard."

Jed barked a laugh and tossed Taffy's reins to Andi. "I'll decide that. Here. Take the reins. But I'm warning you . . ." He laid a hand on the gun in his waistband. "No tricks. You stick close, or else. Understand?"

"Yes," Andi replied through clenched teeth. She gathered up the reins. "I understand perfectly."

Jed reached out and slapped Andi's horse on the rump. "Let's move!"

Taffy took off, with Jed close behind. They rode all afternoon, stopping only long enough to water the horses. Jed led them through scrub oak and gulches filled with thick, scratchy brush. They crossed dry creek beds and urged their horses over hills that grew higher as they neared the mountains. The scorching sun beat down for so long that Andi was sure evening would never come.

"Where are we going?" she asked during one of their brief stops to water the horses. She squatted on the rocks, plunged her hands into the stream, and splashed the cool water onto her face. Then she drank her fill. She wished Jed would let her take off her shoes and stockings so she could wade—even for a minute. She was sweltering in this heat.

Jed looked at her. "We're goin' to Mexico. But first I gotta lose any posse that might be followin' us."

Andi froze, water dripping down her face. "Mexico? I don't want to go to Mexico."

"I ain't askin' you. Now, get outta the water and back on the horse."

"Just a minute more?" she begged. "I'm so hot."

Jed shook his head and scowled. "Let's move."

Andi reluctantly left the stream and climbed onto Taffy. She wished she had something she could let drop—like a small handkerchief or a button—so the posse could track them over the rocky ground. But she couldn't think of one thing. Besides, Jed was watching her too closely. He'd notice if she dropped a shoe or started ripping apart her skirt.

Jed swung into his saddle, and they rode silently for many miles. More than once, Andi looked over to see him regarding her thoughtfully. "What's the matter?" she finally asked. "Why do you keep looking at me like that?"

Jed scratched at his neck and cleared his throat. "Guess I'm feelin' a mite guilty for bringin' you along," he confessed. "'Specially after what your brother did for me in court. He's a good lawyer—mighty fine with all those high-falutin' words." He sighed, and his look pleaded for understanding. "But you gotta understand I had no choice. I'm innocent and I ain't goin' to prison."

"Justin knows you're innocent," Andi said. "He wants to help you. But running off with his sister is *not* a good way to keep him on your side." She smiled to take the sting from her words. "It's not too late to take me back. It would prove your innocence. Trust Justin to—"

"I can't!" Jed cut her off. "So it's no use tryin' to talk me into turnin' around, or any other fool thing. I'm goin' to Mexico, and you're along to make sure I get there. I'm sorry, little lady, but that's the way it's gotta be. Soon as I cross the border, I'll let you go."

"You're just going to ride off and leave me alone?" Andi was aghast. "Don't you care what happens to me? What kind of a man are you?"

"A desperate one."

By evening, Andi was so tired that she could scarcely keep her eyes open, much less stay in the saddle. Twice she drifted off to sleep, but the continual jarring of the horse jerked her awake.

Jed glanced uneasily at her. "You're plumb tuckered out, ain't you?" He pulled his horse to a stop near a secluded grove of scraggly cottonwoods and scrub oak and dismounted. Taffy stopped as well. "Looks like we can't go no further tonight—even if the entire town of Fresno's after us. I sure hope we've thrown any posse off our trail long enough for a decent night's rest."

Andi slid from the saddle and onto the ground in a weary heap.

"This looks as good a place as any," Jed remarked. "Plenty of cover, but enough space to spread out a couple o' bedrolls and graze the horses." He gathered the canteens, saddlebags, and bedrolls into his arms. "Take care of the horses while I set up camp."

Andi didn't move. "I'm too tired. And the saddles are awful heavy."

"Just do it, and do it quick." Jed lugged the gear into the small clearing a few yards away and dumped everything onto the ground. Then he turned back to Andi and planted his hands on his hips. "I'm keepin' you to your promise, remember? No cryin' or faintin' from *you*." He grinned. "Let's see what you're made of."

Andi bit back an angry reply. The man's words sent a hot rush of blood through her that drove her fatigue away, just as Jed had most likely intended. She unsaddled the horses and wrestled with the heavy saddles until they were safely under a tree. Then she collapsed to the ground, spent. She wished with all her heart she could close her eyes, but a little nicker from Taffy reminded her that she hadn't finished her work.

Half asleep, she dragged herself to her feet and made her way back to hobble the horses and unbridle them. Her fingers fumbled in the growing darkness.

Taffy hungrily attacked the dry autumn grass, snorting her displeasure at the shabby care she was receiving tonight. Andi rubbed Taffy's nose as the mare bit off quick, short lengths of grass. "I'm sorry for all this," she whispered. "Things will get better soon, I promise."

The horse shook her mane and snorted. Andi leaned wearily against her soft flank and closed her eyes. Taffy was warm, and her presence was a comfort—a reminder of home. The familiar scent and touch of her friend cheered her, and she sighed. *Thank You, God, for sending Taffy along today to keep me company.*

Jed's gruff command yanked her from her moment of peace. "Come on over here and eat. I don't want you fallin' over from lack of food."

Andi shuffled over. She glanced around at the dark shadows creeping over the campsite and shivered. "I don't suppose there'll be a fire."

He laughed. "Sorry, no."

Andi slid down next to a log and took the food and blanket he offered. She bit into the piece of tough beef and made a face. She hated jerky, but tonight she was hungry enough to eat it without choking. Jed passed her the canteen without a word.

Thankful to wash the salty taste from her mouth, Andi drank quickly and handed the canteen back to her captor. Then she drew the blanket around her shoulders, yawned, and closed her eyes.

A rough shake brought her awake with a jolt.

"Hey, girl. I never caught your name."

Andi pulled the blanket closer. "Why do you care?"

"I'm gittin' kinda tired of callin' you 'girl.' Since we're gonna be partners for a spell, I thought we might get on friendlier terms. You can call me Jed if you like."

"No thanks, mister," she mumbled sleepily. "We may be traveling together, but that sure doesn't make us partners."

Jed scowled. "Suit yourself. Just tryin' to be friendly. But I shoulda known. Well, Miss *Carter*, I reckon you'll be mighty glad of my friendship down in Mexico. I know just enough Mexi-talk to get us by."

"I thought you were going to leave me at the border."

Jed grinned. "Maybe I changed my mind."

"Go away," Andi said, too tired to make sense of Jed's words. "I want to sleep."

"Ain't you the least bit curious to know why I came back to town?"

"No." Andi lay down on the cold, hard ground and curled up into a tight ball. She shivered as the chilly autumn night set in. There was no moonlight to pierce the darkness. Only a handful of stars peeked through the clearing in the trees.

She closed her eyes. Never in her life had she felt so cold, tired, or frightened. She tried to keep her fear inside, but it trickled out between her eyelids in hot, silent tears. A whimper escaped her lips. *Please, God. I know Justin said You'd go with me, but I'm so scared. Take care of me, and please help my brothers find me.*

Suddenly, she felt movement close by. Her eyes flew open. Jed Hatton towered over her, a black shadow against the feeble light of the stars. She caught her breath, frightened to think of what he might do next.

"Don't worry, little lady," he whispered gruffly, gently covering her with his own blanket. He stepped back. "I won't let nothin' bad happen to you."

Andi heard no more.

Chapter Fifteen

A DESPERATE CHANCE

Andi woke with a start and sat up. Dawn was a pale streak in the sky. It took a minute before she remembered where she was and why she'd spent the night on the hard ground. As the memories washed over her, she shuddered and glanced at her captor. He was propped against a large oak tree, snoring. His dirty, unkempt hair hung over his eyes and his gun rested in his lap, his fingers curled loosely around it.

Andi smiled to herself. Here was her chance to escape. Quietly, she got up and made her way over to Taffy, who was standing with the other horse across the campsite. If she could mount her horse without waking Jed, she would be free. Nobody could catch Taffy.

She whispered quieting words to the mare while she unhobbled her. Grasping the creamy mane, she pulled herself smoothly and silently onto Taffy's back. With a gentle pressure, she urged the horse forward.

The sharp click of a gun being cocked broke the early morning silence.

Andi froze.

"Goin' somewhere, little lady?"

Andi turned and faced Jed. He was leaning against the tree, groggy from sleep. "I'm going home," came her quiet reply.

Jed yawned and lowered his gun. With a grunt, he rose to his feet and brushed the hair away from his eyes. "Girl," he said, breaking into a grin, "you sure do beat all." He started toward Taffy, waving his gun at her. "How you plan on ridin' that horse? No reins, no bridle. You just gonna sweet-talk her into takin' you home?"

"This is *my* horse," Andi said. "She'll go wherever I say."

"Do tell!" Jed chuckled. "I expect we're in for some interestin' times together—you and me. You showed real gumption back at the schoolhouse, but don't let it go to your head. Now, get off the horse."

"I'm going home," Andi repeated.

Jed scowled. "Now you listen to me, girl, and listen good. You ain't goin' home. You ain't goin' nowhere 'til I say so." He sighed. "Looks like I'll have to tie you up at night to make sure you stay put."

Andi was outraged. "You just wait, Jed Hatton. My brothers'll catch up with you. They'll take you back to town and you'll hang, because I betcha anything you really *did* murder that man—no matter what Justin says."

Jed shrugged. With his free hand he fished around inside his jacket and pulled out a small, bulging leather pouch. "Know what this is?"

Andi shook her head.

"It's gold dust. *My* gold dust. The baggage clerk got in the way. I had to kill him." He shook the pouch. "This here's the reason I came back to town. I'd hidden it. I need this gold to live on, down in Mexico."

Andi caught her breath. "Then you really *are* guilty!"

Jed smirked.

"But Justin—"

"I had him fooled," said Jed. "I admit your brother's a right smart lawyer. He almost got me off. Got me a prison term instead of a noose. Made it easier for me to escape." He laughed. "Kind of a surprise, ain't it?"

Andi's heart slammed against the inside of her chest. She clenched her fists, too angry to be afraid. Jed had lied to Justin, who had done his best to prove the man's innocence. "You low-down, dirty, rotten, lying—"

"Quit your yappin'," Jed ordered. "You can cuss me out all you want later. Let's eat and be on our way."

Andi shook her head. "I'm not going another step with a killer who lies to his own lawyer."

Jed lowered his gun and marched over to Andi's horse. "You come down off that horse or I'll pull you off."

"No!" Andi shouted in sudden, frantic decision. She reached out and kicked at Jed's gun hand with all her might. The gun flew from his hand and landed on the ground a few feet away. She pressed her heels into Taffy's sides as hard as she could. The horse bolted.

Andi heard Jed swear and scramble for his gun. She paid no attention. She had to ride far and fast.

"Come back here, you fool kid, or I'll shoot! I mean it!"

Never! She'd take her chances. Maybe he was bluffing. She glanced back. The last thing she heard was Jed Hatton shouting at her. The last thing she saw was a bright flash.

Andi woke to the sound of a man's frantic pleading. "You gotta wake up, girl. It was an accident. Just a warning shot. I never meant to hurt you. You gotta believe me." He reached out and gave her a shake. "You understand? I didn't mean to do it."

Searing pain shot through Andi's head at the sudden movement. She tried to make sense of the man's words. What was he going on about? Where was she? Why did everything hurt so much?

"Girl!" The terror in the man's voice frightened Andi into opening her eyes. A dirty, unshaven face loomed just inches above her face. When he saw she was awake, he let out a long, deep sigh and sat back. "Thank God you're not dead." Then he tossed a blanket over her and rose to his feet. "I hate t' leave you, but I got no choice. Your brother ain't likely to forgive me for this. If I stay here, I'm a dead man." He reached down and laid a rough palm against her cheek. His voice softened. "I'm sorry, girl. I really am."

Then he mounted his horse and galloped away.

No! Don't go! Andi wanted to scream, but she couldn't make the words come. She sat up, and pain as sharp as a knife stabbed the inside of her head, making her gasp. She clutched her head with both hands and groaned.

Her stomach lurched violently at the unexpected movement, and what was left of her meager supper suddenly spewed onto the ground in front of her. She swallowed and took a deep breath. Then another. She lowered her hands and was shocked to see the fingers of her left hand covered with bright red blood.

What happened? It hurt so much to think. Fighting back another wave of nausea, she glanced around the campsite. The scruffy-looking man had certainly left in a hurry. A saddle lay abandoned under a tree; saddlebags and blankets were scattered across the ground. A canteen hung suspended from the branch of an old scrub oak.

"Why did he leave? Where am I?" Andi squeezed her eyes shut and tried to think. But it was no use. Her mind could focus on nothing but the agony in her head. She couldn't remember where she was or how she got here, or who the man on the galloping horse was. In fact, she couldn't remember anything at all. It was as if someone had slammed a door shut in her head and locked it tight.

A sharp *crack* from the bushes across the campsite propelled Andi to her feet, heart pounding. Then she cried out and collapsed to the ground. Her stomach roiled. Quickly, she scuttled backward into the brush and waited, clenching her teeth against the pain.

To her astonishment, a golden horse broke into the clearing, trotted up to Andi, and nickered a greeting. Then the mare lowered her head and blew out, gently nibbling Andi's hair and nuzzling her in a way that made her feel warm all over.

The joy of finding another living creature made Andi forget her pain for the moment. She crawled from her hiding place and reached up to stroke the mare's soft nose. "I don't know where you came from, but I'm glad you're here," she whispered. The horse nickered again and nudged her, as if encouraging her to stand and mount up.

Andi staggered to her feet, leaning against the horse for support. Her head throbbed. "I can't," she apologized softly, sliding to the ground in defeat. She knew she should try to find help, yet all she really wanted to do was lie down so her head would stop pounding. "Don't wander off," she told the mare. Then she reached for the blankets, crawled into the brush, and curled up on the ground. Immediately, the pain lessened. With a sigh, she closed her eyes and slept.

The sound of approaching riders startled Andi awake some time later. She didn't know how long she'd slept, but the sun was no longer overhead. Dusk had settled in, casting long, gray shadows over the campsite.

Andi sat up at the sound. It was a mistake. Her head instantly began pounding again. But at least her stomach didn't protest. She looked around for the horse and found her munching contentedly on some dry grass a few yards away. The mare was half-hidden in the shadows. For that, Andi was grateful. She huddled on the blanket and waited to see what would happen.

The sound of hoofbeats grew nearer, then stopped.

"This way," a loud voice boomed. "It looks like they made camp here last night. At least we're on the right track."

There was a rustling sound, and six men appeared in the clearing. Andi watched them warily from her secluded spot in the brush. None resembled the scruffy man who had abandoned her. These men were strangers.

"What happened here?" A tall man wearing a sheriff's badge

yanked the canteen from the deadwood. "Looks like they left in a hurry. Why would they leave all this behind?"

No one answered him.

"Over here!" one of the deputies hollered. "I found a horse. It's the palomino."

Andi didn't know what to do. They'd found the horse. It wouldn't be long before they found—

"Andi!"

The sound of the astonished voice just beyond the brush brought her around. She locked gazes with a sandy-haired young man.

He grinned. "I'm sure glad to see *you*. Come on out and tell us what happened. Where's Jed?" He reached out a helping hand and called to the others. "Over here, Justin, Chad!"

Andi shrank from the man's offer. Things were happening too fast. Who were these people? Who was Jed?

"What's the matter?" The young man's smile faded. "Justin! There's blood all over the place."

Justin hurried over. His gaze swept over the scene, and his jaw tightened.

"Go away," Andi whispered to this newest intruder.

Justin backed off. "Take it easy, honey. We didn't mean to frighten you. We've come to take you home."

Home? Andi stared at Justin. He looked vaguely familiar, but she couldn't place him. *I should know him*, she thought. *But it's too much work to remember.*

"Does your head hurt?" he asked.

"Yes."

"Could I take a look at it? I'll be very careful. I promise." He smiled and reached out his hand. "Let me help you."

Andi considered. She knew she couldn't hide in the bushes any longer. Night was coming on, and she hurt. This man had a gentle voice. She relaxed and placed her hand into his.

Justin guided her into the clearing and knelt down beside her. Carefully, he brushed aside the dark, blood-soaked tangles, exposing a finger-length gash along the side of her head. It oozed bright red blood.

The others crowded around for a closer look.

At the sight of the wound, Chad drew a sharp breath. "He shot her, Justin." His voice shook with anger. "Your *innocent* client shot our sister. What kind of man would—?" He broke off. "I'll kill him myself."

Andi looked around at her rescuers. They were her brothers? Why didn't she recognize them?

"Did Jed shoot you?" Justin asked.

Andi shivered. "I don't know." She turned a frightened gaze on him. "I don't remember anything." She started to cry. "I only know my head hurts and I'm scared, and . . . and . . . I want to go home."

"That's why we're here," Justin said in a soothing voice. He took a blanket and wrapped it tightly around her shoulders. "You're safe now. We'll have you home in no time, in your own bed, and you'll have medicine to make your head stop hurting. How does that sound?"

Andi regarded Justin warily. "Are you . . . are you really my brother?"

Justin nodded and lifted her from the ground. "Of course I am, honey."

Andi leaned her head against Justin's shoulder. Although she didn't recognize this stranger, it felt good to be picked up and held by him. It felt *right*.

She closed her eyes. "Take me home."

Chapter Sixteen

STARTING OVER

The sound of murmuring voices brought Andi back to consciousness. She opened her eyes and noticed that a warm, cozy bed had replaced the cold ground. The dreadful pounding in her head had been exchanged for a dull ache, which was bearable. A single lamp burned on a table, bathing the room in a soft yellow glow.

"Well, Dr. Weaver?" Andi turned her head toward the voice. An attractive older woman stood in earnest conversation with a tall, gray-haired man. The woman's long, silver-streaked blond hair hung down her back in a loose braid. Her worry-filled blue eyes searched the doctor's face for an answer.

"I'll be honest with you, Elizabeth," came the quiet reply. "A gunshot wound is always serious. I cleaned and stitched it up the best I could. Let's hope it doesn't become infected."

"What about her memory?"

The doctor sighed. "Amnesia's a funny thing. She could have lost her memory from the head injury or even from the emotional shock she's experienced." He shrugged to indicate his helplessness. "I have no idea which it is. Frankly, it wouldn't matter if I did. There's no treatment. Just give her lots of rest, good food, and plenty of love. Surround her with familiar things, and who knows? She could regain her memory tomorrow—just like that." He snapped his fingers.

"Is it possible she might never regain it?"

The doctor held up his hand. "Please, Elizabeth. One worry at a time. There's no sense borrowing trouble. You know what the Scriptures say: 'Sufficient unto the day is the evil thereof.'" He reached out and laid a gentle hand on her arm. "You've had plenty of evil for one day, I think. Just thank God they found her at all."

Elizabeth nodded.

Dr. Weaver closed his bag and turned to go. "See that someone stays with her until she wakes up. I'll come by tomorrow afternoon." He patted her on the shoulder. "You need some rest."

"Thank you for coming out here at such a late hour, John."

"Think nothing of it. We've seen Andrea through everything from croup to measles. We'll see her through this, too." He smiled. "I'll let myself out."

Elizabeth turned back to Andi, who quickly shut her eyes. She didn't want anyone to know she was awake. She wasn't ready to talk to anybody, not even to this beautiful, sad-faced woman who must be her mother.

She felt the cool, tender touch of the woman's hand against her cheek and nearly jumped. Then the bed covers were tucked gently around her. A light kiss brushed across the bandage on her head.

"Andrea," a soft voice whispered, "I know you can't hear me. Even if you could, you don't know me. But it's all right. When I learned you were gone, I cried out to the Lord and He brought you back this far. That's all that matters for now. I know He'll bring you the rest of the way in His own time."

After a pause, the voice continued. "Mr. Foster says you were brave—the bravest in the class. You saved Virginia's life. Of course, it doesn't mean much to you now, sweetheart, but in time . . ." Andi heard the rustling of paper. "I'll read aloud for a while. Perhaps the sound of my voice will trigger a memory somewhere."

Andi lay still, perfectly content. She could have listened to her mother's soothing voice for the rest of the night, but the warmth of the bed enveloped her once again, and she fell asleep.

"Well, young lady," Dr. Weaver boomed cheerfully, "it looks like you're on the mend." He dropped the soiled white cloth, which had served as a bandage for the past several days, into the basin. "You won't be needing this any longer. No bleeding, no fever, no redness. Everything is coming along nicely. Patients like you make me feel good about my profession." He squeezed Andi's arm and stood up from the bed. "You can get up and return to a few quiet activities. In another week or two, you'll be as good as new."

"Not quite," Andi said.

Dr. Weaver frowned. "Don't be impatient, Andrea. Give yourself time to remember."

Elizabeth lowered herself onto the bed, where Andi sat propped against the headboard. She picked up one of her hands and held it between her own. "Sweetheart, do you remember anything about the accident? Anything at all?"

Andi grew quiet. She stared past her mother, past the doctor, and through the French doors leading outside to the balcony. She felt dazed. Trying to remember was hard work. It was easier to let her mind wander to less important matters, like what she was having for supper tonight. She found herself doing that a lot lately.

"Andrea," her mother prompted.

"I remember the blood." Andi shivered. "I remember how much it hurt." She closed her eyes and drew in a deep breath. "I remember a scruffy-looking man talking to me." She opened her eyes. "Sometimes I see him yelling at me, telling me to do something I don't want to do. I'm sitting on a horse. I remember him galloping away. I don't remember anything else."

"Well, that's something." Dr. Weaver winked his encouragement. He picked up his bag and turned to leave. "I'll drop by the beginning of next week to take out the stitches. If you need anything before then, just send word."

Elizabeth nodded and rose from the bed. "I must see to supper, Andrea. We'd like you to join us downstairs tonight."

"Do I have to?" She didn't want to go downstairs. She didn't want to sit at the table and feel her sister's and brothers' pity. She could see it in their eyes and hear it in their forced attempts at cheerfulness.

"It will be our last supper as a family for a while. Chad and Mitch are heading out with the men tomorrow to bring the stock down from the high country. It will be a couple of weeks before they return. We've missed you at meals, sweetheart."

Andi gave in. "All right."

Her mother blew her a kiss before she left the room. "You rest now. I'll send someone to fetch you when supper's ready."

Rest. Andi grimaced. *That's all I've been doing for days. So, why am I always tired?* She lay back against the pillows and stared at the ceiling. Within minutes, she was asleep.

"Andi?" A quiet whisper brought her awake. She sat up, curious. Standing outside her door was a girl not much older than herself. She had huge brown eyes and black hair pulled tightly into two shiny braids.

"Who are you?" Andi asked.

"Rosa. My parents work for your family. So do I. *Mamá* would not let me talk to you until today, after the doctor left." She lowered her voice. "But many times I sneaked in while you were sleeping, to pray God might heal you." She broke into a beautiful smile. "And *gracias a Dios*—He heard my prayers."

This brought a smile to Andi's lips. "Thank you." She patted the bed. "Sit down and visit with me awhile."

"Actually," Rosa said, sitting down on the bed and slipping into rapid Spanish, "the *señora* sent me up here to tell you it's almost suppertime. She thought maybe you'd like me to help you dress and show you the way to the dining room."

The look on Rosa's face was so hopeful that Andi consented. She allowed Rosa to pick out a dress for her and brush her hair.

"There," Rosa announced a few minutes later. "*Mucho mejor.*"

Andi studied her reflection in the mirror. She didn't think she looked much better. The dark-haired stranger staring back at her looked frightened and lost. The scattering of freckles across her nose stood out in sharp contrast to her pale face. There was no sparkle in her wide blue eyes. She reached up and carefully pulled her hair back. With her other hand, she traced the ugly row of stitches along the side of her head. The tiny black threads tickled her fingers. She shuddered and let her hair fall forward to hide the sight.

"When you return to school," Rosa offered cheerfully, "everyone will want to see it, *no?*" Her voice grew quiet when Andi didn't answer. "*Lo siento,*" she mumbled in apology.

"It's all right." Andi stood up. "I guess I'd better go downstairs."

Rosa left Andi at the dining room and disappeared toward the kitchen to help her mother.

"Well, young lady," Justin greeted her, hurrying to her side, "don't you look pretty tonight!" He led her to a place next to Melinda and pulled out the chair.

"We're having your favorite supper," Melinda said. "Can you guess what it is?"

Andi shook her head and sat down.

"Try," Mitch encouraged. "What's the first thing that comes to your mind when you think of food?"

"Fried chicken, mashed potatoes and gravy, and . . . and . . . biscuits and jam?"

"That's exactly right, Andi," Justin said with an encouraging wink. "You remembered."

At that moment Nila and Rosa appeared with the meal. Fried chicken it was, along with many things Andi had not guessed: a heaping platter of golden corn-on-the-cob, a dish overflowing with green beans, two pans of fresh peach cobbler. A spark of hope raced through her at the sight. She smiled shyly at Justin and picked up her fork.

It was a little awkward talking to a roomful of strangers, but they were nice strangers, Andi decided. And the food was delicious. She only had to be polite and not spill her milk or do anything else to embarrass herself. Soon she would be allowed to return to the security of her room.

"Your friends miss you," Justin remarked, buttering a biscuit. "They paid a visit to my office this afternoon. They want to know when you're coming back to school."

Andi froze, a chicken leg halfway to her mouth. "Never."

"Never is a long time, Andrea," her mother remarked.

"Cory asked if he could come out to the ranch to see you," Justin continued as if his sister hadn't spoken. "I told him to wait a few more days."

"I don't want any visitors."

"Come on, Andi," Chad broke in. "Couldn't you just talk to him? Maybe you'll recognize him."

"No!" she insisted fiercely, slamming the drumstick onto her plate. "I'm not ready." She reached for her milk with a shaking hand and tipped it over. The contents spilled across the table and into Mitch's lap. With a startled yelp, he sprang from his chair. Andi burst into tears.

"This started out as a quiet, enjoyable supper together," Elizabeth reminded her family. "Please do not spoil it."

"I'm sorry, Andi," Chad apologized, flinging his napkin in Mitch's direction. "I won't mention it again."

Andi wiped her eyes. She picked up her piece of chicken and

pretended to listen as her brothers talked about the roundup for the rest of the meal. She looked at each family member, trying to remember them. It was no use. When supper was over, they remained as much a group of strangers as they'd been since she received the injury.

Chapter Seventeen

A TIME TO REMEMBER

P lease!" Andi pleaded. "I want to go home. We've come far enough. Please! Let me go home."

A rough voice laughed. "Nuthin' doin', little lady. As long as I've got you, nobody will dare follow me."

Andi felt anger and fear rise up inside her. She curled her fingers tightly around the horse's mane and shouted at a scruffy-looking, dark-eyed stranger. "I'm leaving."

An iron grip closed around her arm and tried to yank her from her horse.

Andi screamed. "Let me go! Let me—"

"Andrea. Wake up." A firm voice cut through Andi's dream. Her mother had her by the shoulders, gently shaking her awake. "You're dreaming again," she said, lowering herself to her daughter's side.

With a gasp, Andi sat up and threw her arms around her mother, not caring if the woman was still a stranger. She took several deep breaths to still her pounding heart. Slowly, she relaxed as her mother gently stroked her hair and spoke soothing words.

"Another nightmare?" Elizabeth asked.

Andi nodded.

"Can you tell me about it?"

"It was so real," Andi whispered. "So dreadful. I—I think I'm starting to remember." Then she shivered. "But I don't want these kinds of memories. I'd rather not remember at all."

"You don't mean that, sweetheart."

"I do. I'm having more and more bad dreams."

At that moment, Justin poked a tousled head into the room. "Is everything all right in here?" He smiled at Andi, but he looked at their mother for the answer to his question.

"Another bad dream," Elizabeth explained.

Andi couldn't help noticing the concerned glance that passed between her mother and her brother. They knew. No matter how hard Andi tried to keep her worries to herself, Justin and her mother had somehow figured out she was not getting better.

Except for her dreams, Andi had remembered nothing of importance in the three weeks since she was injured. She was frightened, lonely, and short-tempered. Her only activity consisted of riding Taffy around the yard or in the nearest pasture. The one time she'd ridden up into the foothills, she'd lost her way and wandered around for hours before finally giving up and letting her horse find the way home. Since then, she wasn't allowed to go anywhere on the ranch alone. Not anywhere! She wanted to scream in frustration. Instead, she found herself in tears most of the time.

"Why don't we head to the kitchen for a midnight snack?" Justin suggested brightly.

Andi shook her head. "I'm not hungry."

"Sure you are," Justin insisted. "We'll heat some chocolate and talk a bit." He turned to his mother. "I learned something important today. I wasn't sure when I should bring it up, but now seems like a good time."

"All right." Elizabeth rose from the bed and held out her hand to Andi. "Come on, sweetheart. Let's find something to eat and see what your brother has to say."

Over cups of steaming chocolate and a platter of sugar cookies, Andi listened to Justin's discovery.

"Sheriff Tate dropped by my office today. He brought a wire from down south that says Jed Hatton was captured." He paused.

"And?" Elizabeth urged.

"They're bringing him back to Fresno by train. He should be here in a couple of days." Justin lowered his cup of chocolate to the table. "Russ told me that Jed shot up a couple of deputies while trying to escape. That doesn't sound like an innocent man to me." He let out a deep, regretful sigh. "How could I have been so mistaken? If I hadn't believed in his innocence, I never would have defended him. He might have gotten a different sentence. Then he wouldn't have returned to town and—" He glanced at Andi, who was listening with interest.

"Don't do this to yourself, Justin," Elizabeth said. "What's done is done. Just tell me why on earth the man's coming back to Fresno. I'd prefer to see him far away and safely behind bars."

"When I heard about his capture, I asked if he could be brought here before going on to prison."

"Whatever for?"

"Because we can't go on like this. It's been three weeks and Andi's no better." Justin sighed. "I have an idea. It may not be a very good one, but it's worth a try. Maybe if Andi saw Jed, if she could hear him talk, something would trigger her memory and bring it back." He caught Andi's startled reaction and smiled. "You're so close, honey. You're almost remembering."

"What if something goes wrong?" Elizabeth asked. "What if talking to Jed pushes her memories deeper?"

"Well, it certainly can't get much worse. I say we give it a try."

Elizabeth glanced at her daughter. "Andrea?" Andi looked up. "What do you think? Do you want to take a chance on remembering by confronting the man who hurt you?"

Andi bit her lip and stared at her quickly cooling chocolate. The image of a dirty, unshaven face loomed up in front of her, and she shivered. She wanted to forget that face, not see it for real. She started to shake her head, but chanced a look at her brother. Justin's eyes were filled with deep regret and sorrow, as if he blamed himself for what had happened to her. Yet he always put on a cheerful face around her and tried to make her happy. Couldn't she do this one thing for him?

"I'm scared," she said.

"I know you are," Justin coaxed. "But he can't hurt you any longer. He's behind bars."

Andi let out a deep breath. She didn't want to do it, but she was so tired of looking at her family and seeing only strangers. She nodded slowly.

"Good girl." Justin broke into a genuine smile. "I'll be with you the whole time. We'll see this through together."

"We've come to see Jed Hatton," Justin announced when he and Andi walked into the sheriff's office two days later.

"I hope you know what you're doing, Justin." The sheriff waved a greeting to Andi, who didn't return it. "He's not exactly in a cooperative mood back there. Are you sure this is a good idea?"

"No, I'm not sure it's a good idea. But it's the only idea I have. Now c'mon, Russ, let me see him."

The sheriff opened the door that led to the jail cells. "Hatton," he called out, "you've got visitors. It's your lawyer."

"He ain't my lawyer no more."

"Well, he's visiting you just the same."

Justin stepped around the sheriff and motioned Andi to stay where she was. "It's good to see you alive, Jed," he said.

Jed snorted.

Justin walked down the corridor and stopped in front of Jed's cell. "It is. I really am glad to see you. Do you know why you've made the stop here in Fresno?"

"Nope. Don't care, neither."

"It's so you can clear your conscience before you head on to prison."

"Huh? Don't talk in riddles."

Justin sighed. "All right, Jed. Here it is. I defended you in court. Got you a prison sentence instead of a noose. I did my best for you because I believed you were innocent. And I continued to believe, even when I heard you'd escaped. I wanted to help you by going after an appeal, but you wouldn't give me a chance. Instead, you repaid me by kidnapping my sister and leaving her to die out in the middle of nowhere." He took a step forward and gripped the bars of the cell. His knuckles turned white.

Jed stumbled backward, clearly shocked. His voice dropped to a whisper. "She's dead?"

"No. We found her in time, no thanks to you." Justin shook his head. "You know what, Jed? My brother Chad would love to get his hands on you for what you did. I'm tempted to let him, but he might have to stand in line. It won't take long before this town finds out you're here."

"What do you want from me?" Jed growled.

Justin stepped back and let his hands drop to his sides. "I want you to help bring back Andi's memory. She can't remember anything up to the day we found her. The gunshot wound to her head is the cause."

"So? Where do I come in?"

"Talk to her. Help her relive the last few minutes before her . . ." Justin paused. *"Accident."*

"It *was* an accident," Jed said. "Just a warning shot to scare her into coming back. I never meant to hit her. When she fell off her horse, I brought her back to camp and tended her the best I could. But I was scared, lawyer. You don't know *how* scared. I figured you'd shoot me on sight, so I took off. I meant no harm to the girl. You gotta believe me."

"Andi, come here," Justin called.

Andi joined her brother in front of the cell. She looked up at Jed and felt herself fill with dread. The man behind these bars was clean-shaven, not scruffy and dirty like the face in her memory. His hair was combed neatly to the side.

"Do you recognize him?" Justin wanted to know.

"I don't know."

"I sure remember you, little lady," Jed said. "I'm glad you're all right. It was real scary seein' you lying there so still."

Andi shook her head at the man and backed away. She might not recognize his face, but his voice struck a chord deep inside. She knew she'd heard it somewhere before. The brief image of a man looking up at her and talking flashed through her head and she winced. "No," she whispered.

Jed grinned. "You sure had a lot of pluck to sass me the way you did—'specially when I was holdin' a gun on you. You were sittin' up on that horse all keen on runnin' off. Said your brothers were gonna catch me, and I'd hang. That wasn't nice, gal. You should've stuck with me. We'd have been over the border by now, and I would've let you go—more'n likely."

Andi looked to Justin, who motioned her to keep talking to Jed. But she didn't want to. She'd heard enough of his voice. "Justin, it's not working. Can we go home now?" She turned away from the cell.

Jed's voice stopped her in her tracks. "Goin' somewhere, little lady?"

Andi caught her breath. She whirled around to face Jed, startled by the familiar words. A chill raced up and down her spine when she realized she had heard those very words before. They had burned themselves into her mind. In an instant, she was back at the campsite. Just like in her nightmares. Her heart beat faster. A picture formed in her head of Jed sitting against a tree, gun raised. Suddenly, it was crystal clear, and Andi knew that the words she spoke next, she had spoken before.

"*I'm going home!*" she cried out. Her memory returned in such a flood that it made her stagger backward. Justin caught her, but she pushed away from him and walked right up to the bars of Jed's cell. "I remember!" Andi shouted at him, angry now. "I remember everything. Why did you shoot me? I only wanted to go home, and you wouldn't let me." She whipped around to face Justin and the sheriff. "I remember something else, too. He told me he really did kill Mr. Slater. He said he did it for the gold dust."

Jed whistled. "You sure got your memory back in a hurry, girl."

Andi ignored him. She threw her arms around Justin and hugged him. "I know you, Justin. I really do." She didn't know whether to laugh or cry, so she did both. Happy tears poured down her face. She brushed them away and hugged her brother tighter. She heard him whisper, "Thank God."

Sheriff Tate echoed Justin's words. "Thank God is right. It's been a long three weeks—for everyone." When Andi looked at him, the sheriff had tears in his eyes. "It's good to have you back, Andi," he said solemnly, reaching out his hand.

Andi took the sheriff's large, calloused hand and squeezed it. "Thank you, Sheriff. I'm awfully glad to *be* back."

"Don't hear nobody thankin' *me*," Jed grumbled.

Justin and the sheriff escorted Andi down the hall and back into the office.

"So," Sheriff Tate said, locking the corridor door. "Now that you've got your memory back, what's the first thing you're going to do?"

Andi exchanged a quick glance with Justin. There were so many things she wanted to do, but mostly she wanted to see the rest of her family.

Before she could answer, Justin spoke up. "Why, she's going back to school tomorrow." He grinned at his sister. "Isn't that right, Andi?"

Andi gulped. School?

Chapter Eighteen

BACK TO SCHOOL

I feel like I've swallowed a thousand butterflies," Andi said when she saw the schoolhouse the following morning. "I really don't think I'm ready for this."

"Sure you are," Justin assured her. "After all you've been through, how scary can walking into a roomful of your classmates be?"

"Plenty scary." She snatched the reins from Justin's hands and brought the buggy to an abrupt halt. "By now they've most likely read the *Expositor*'s fanciful account of what happened. I'll have to listen to an earful of questions, when all I want is to forget the whole thing."

Justin took back the reins and urged the horse into a walk. "I know. But Fresno's a small town. Saving Virginia's life is big news. Better learn to accept the attention gracefully."

Andi squirmed. Easier said than done.

Justin brought the buggy to a standstill in front of the schoolyard and motioned Andi and Rosa out. "Go on. It won't be as hard as you think. I promise."

Andi stepped down from the buggy and clasped Rosa's hand. "Let's slip into the schoolhouse before anybody sees us."

Rosa's eyes opened wide, and she laughed. "*¡Eso es imposible!*"

Andi realized how right her friend was the minute she stepped foot in the schoolyard crowded with students, all laughing and running and waiting for the first bell to ring. She looked around with the eyes of an outsider. How strange it felt! Some of the little boys were involved in a rousing game of tug-of-war. Cory and the older boys were deep in conference around the water barrel near the side of the building. She watched one of them put a small object into the dipper. A frog, no doubt. A small grin cracked her face. She would make sure she didn't go after the first drink at recess.

She glanced at the small clusters of girls scattered across the yard. The primary girls were jumping rope and playing as loudly as the little boys, arms clasped tightly around each other as they stood waiting for their turns. The oldest girls, with their ankle-length skirts and their hair carefully pinned up, whispered among themselves near the steps. The girls nearest Andi's age stood by the old oak tree, taking turns on the swing hanging from a high, thick branch.

Then she noticed Virginia Foster watching the group from a distance. Virginia took a few halting steps toward the swing, hesitated, and turned back. She saw Andi, and her eyes widened in surprise. Picking up her skirt, she clattered hastily up the porch steps and disappeared into the schoolhouse.

"What in the world?" Andi wondered aloud.

A shout prevented her from following Virginia into the building. "Andi!" Rachel Cooper squealed, leaping from the swing in obvious delight. "You're back!"

The children swarmed around Andi. To her surprise, her uneasiness melted away at the sound of her classmates welcoming her back to school—just as Justin had promised. In response to her friends' eager questions, she found herself sharing not only her story, but also showing off her scar. The little girls covered their mouths and made faces at the sight. *Oohs* and *aahs* of admiration burst from the older boys and girls. Even the school bully, Johnny Wilson, seemed impressed.

"I've gotta hand it to you, Andi," he admitted grudgingly. "You've got plenty of gumption, if nothing else."

"You should've been here when Mr. Foster came to," Maggie piped up. "He nearly went mad with fear when he found out you

135

were gone. I think he figured your family was going to blame him for what happened."

Jack Goodwin laughed. "Well, one good thing's come from all this. Mr. Foster's sure been a lot nicer these past few weeks. Nobody but Johnny's been thrashed for days."

Everyone laughed—except Johnny.

The first bell rang, breaking up the curious crowd and calling them to class.

Cory hung back and plucked Andi on the sleeve. "Golly, Andi, I just thought of something. You could've made heaps of money."

"What are you talking about?"

"You could've charged the kids to let them look at your gunshot scar. You know, sort of like a peep show—a penny a peek."

"Cory, that's awful!" Then she noticed his mischievous grin and started laughing.

By the time Andi entered the classroom, she felt completely at ease. She headed for the desk she shared with Rosa and slipped into her seat. Gently, she brushed her palm across the top of her desk and smiled. It felt good to be back. It really did. She lifted the lid and reached for her books. Her hand curled around a long, wriggling shape.

Andi jerked her hand back. "There's something in my desk," she told Rosa. Carefully, she peeked under the lid. A pair of small beady eyes stared back. A tongue lashed out.

"Welcome back, Andi," Cory whispered over her shoulder. "It's only Clyde."

Andi slammed the desktop shut and whirled on Cory. "I'm gonna wrap this snake around your neck and—"

"School is in session, Miss Carter."

Andi sat up straight and turned around. She swallowed uneasily. "Yes, sir." She waited for the schoolmaster to scold her or order her to the front of the class to whack her palms for talking after the tardy bell rang. He did neither. He just looked at her.

Andi squirmed. "Am I in trouble?"

Mr. Foster came around to the front of his desk. He crossed his arms over his chest, shook his head, and said, "No, Miss Carter. Not this time."

Andi didn't know what to think. Why was he looking at her so keenly?

"It's good to see you're well enough to attend school," Mr. Foster said at last. He held up a hand to prevent Andi from replying. With his other hand he picked up a folded newspaper from his desk. "It is not my intention to embarrass you," he continued, "but I want to read the story that appeared in this week's *Expositor* for the benefit of the class."

Andi stared at her desktop. Her cheeks burned with embarrassment. Once more she had to listen to the account of her ". . . dangerous but courageous decision to leave the safety of her classroom and journey into the unknown to save the life of a schoolmate," as Mr. Foster so eloquently read. Thankfully, it was short.

He put down the paper. "Quite a different story from the one the paper ran last month, isn't it?"

A hard knot settled in Andi's stomach. Would he *never* forgive her for almost trampling him? Her delight in returning to school began to dissolve.

Mr. Foster continued. "I admit we've had our differences, Miss Carter. You do not easily conform to the rules of propriety, and it has brought you no end of trouble this term." He paused and took a deep breath. "However, your willingness to take my daughter's place made me realize that what I interpreted as defiance and brashness was in reality courage and strength of character. I can never repay you for what you did for my family. I can only thank you from the bottom of my heart." His expression twisted into a sudden and unexpected smile. "What I'm trying to say is, I'm proud to have you as my student, Andrea Carter. Welcome back."

The knot in Andi's stomach melted away, replaced by a warm glow. She tentatively returned Mr. Foster's smile. "Thank you, sir." Now, if only he'd give the day's assignments and move on. She'd had about all the attention she could stomach.

But Mr. Foster wasn't finished. "Miss Foster, you may come forward at this time."

Virginia rose from her seat and glided up the aisle to the front of the classroom. Slowly she turned around, clasped her small hands in front of her skirt, and faced Andi. She looked pale, but when she opened her mouth, her words came out clear and steady. "I've been practicing what I'm going to say for days—ever since I saw you leave the classroom with that outlaw. It should have been me. It *would* have been me if you hadn't jumped up and did what you did." She swallowed. Hard. "Father says you probably saved my life. I want to say 'thank you.'"

Andi waited. Would Virginia also make things right about the stallion and apologize for the lies she'd told? When no more words came, Andi simply said, "You're welcome."

Virginia gave Andi a slight nod, curtsied to her father, and started for her seat.

Mr. Foster frowned, as though Virginia's words were not exactly what he had expected. "Is that all, Miss Foster? You've nothing to add?"

Virginia stopped. She gave her father a puzzled look. "I—I don't think so, sir."

Mr. Foster grunted. "What about your part in the scuffle a few weeks back?"

"Oh!" Virginia's pale cheeks turned pink. "Of course it was wrong of me to slap you, Andrea," she said quickly. "My mother says a lady *never* resorts to physical displays of anger. I apologize."

"And the lying?" Mr. Foster's voice was firm.

"Father!"

"All of it, daughter."

She sighed. "I cannot ride a horse. I'm sorry I led you to believe I could."

Clearly humiliated, Virginia bowed her head and shuffled back to her seat.

Poor Virginia, Andi thought, recognizing her downcast spirit. *It must be hard admitting her faults in front of her father and the entire class.* She caught Virginia's skirt as she passed. "It's all right, Virginia," she whispered. "I forgive you. And—and if you like, I can teach you how to ride."

Virginia paused. "Thank you," she said quietly. Then she raised her head and smiled at Andi. A tear trickled down her cheek. "Thank you very much."

And this time Andi knew she meant it.

Mr. Foster nodded and reached for the classroom Bible.

Of course, Andi *should* have been listening to the Scripture reading. It was all about the Golden Rule—"Such a fitting topic for this morning," the teacher commented between verses. But Andi's mind was not on the inspiring words the teacher was reading. All she could think was, *What am I going to do about Cory's snake?*

To read more about Susan K. Marlow's adventures or to contact her, e-mail susankmarlow@kregel.com.